A Bug Collection

A Bug Collection

short stories

Melody Mansfield

XENO

Book design and layout by Skyler Schulze
Cover design by Rebecca Buhler

Library of Congress Cataloging-in-Publication Data

Mansfield, Melody.
 [Works. Selections]
 A Bug Collection : short stories / Melody Mansfield.—First Edition.
   pages cm
 Includes bibliographical references and index.
 ISBN 978-1-939096-00-5 (alk. paper)
 I. Title.
 PS3613.A5763B84 2013
 813'.6—dc23
                    2013016684

The National Endowment for the Arts, the Los Angeles County Arts Commission, the Los Angeles Department of Cultural Affairs, the City of Pasadena Cultural Affairs Division, Sony Pictures Entertainment, and the Dwight Stuart Youth Fund partially support Red Hen Press.

First Edition
XENO Books is an imprint of Red Hen Press, Pasadena, CA
www.redhen.org/xeno

Acknowledgments

To the administration at Milken Community High School, with special thanks to Rennie Wrubel, Roger Fuller, and Kimberly Schwartz for their vision and support, and for helping me find time to write as well as teach. Thanks also to my very supportive friends and colleagues at Milken as well as to my students, past and present, who have always had faith in the bugs.

To Red Hen Press editors, Kate Gale and Mark Cull, along with their assistants, Ashley Ellis, Rosemary McGuinness, Billy Goldstein, and Gabriela Morales who worked with me from start to finish to polish and promote this collection.

To my personal muses, Debra Sokolow, a talented artist who encourages everything I do, and Jane St. Clair, a gifted writer and musician who collaborated with me to create *A Bug Collection: The Musical*.

To Thais Miller, former student and published author, as well as to Martha Wright and Sue Borst, who have all been instrumental in launching this collection. And to my many other dear friends and sisters—Lisa, the Dianes, Rhonda, Kathy, Chris, Ellen, Felicia, Laurie, and Lynn—who responded so quickly and wholeheartedly when I asked for help.

To my wonderful Vermont College friends, Diane Lefer, Dan Jaffe, Jane Bradley, Terry Ann Thaxton, and Mary Clyde, who took time out of their busy writing/ teaching schedules to send me their kind and eloquent words.

To Kitsune Books editor, Anne Petty, who had to drop out of the project but who wrote to tell me: "We are in love with your little book." I wish you health, Anne, and every happiness.

To my daughters, Shawna and Sarah, for their unwavering love for both me and my bugs, and to my husband, Jerry Mansfield—always my first reader and always on my side.

And with grateful acknowledgments to the editors of the following publications where some of these stories were accepted or originally appeared:

Ascent Aspirations, "Earthworm Reveries," "Victoria's Secret"; *Fickle Muses*, "The Rape of Persephone"; *Literary Dilettantes*, "Portrait of the Artist as a Young Millipede"; *nthposition*, "Mantis Prayers"; *Pedestal*, "A Day in September"; *Thought Magazine*, "The Education of Old Dan," "Fireflies of the Vanities"; and *Wild Violet*, "Ephemeroptera."

for
Marlon, Avery, Atticus, Seleia, and Owen

And to my friends and students, past and present,
at Milken Community High School

Contents

A Bug Collection

Ephemeroptera

"They lied to us?" May stood lightly on the mud. She worried, for the first time, that the viscous earth might catch at her delicate tarsi and pull her down into an early grave. "All of it was just a lie?"

Old Dan nodded. "'Fraid so," he said. "I thought you'd want to hear it from me."

Manny stretched and retracted his long front legs. "But I don't understand," he said. "Why lie about it? Why feed us all that crap about our 'bright and glorious' futures?"

Old Dan rolled some of the muddy material into a ball, then stopped himself. Probably insensitive to keep on working at a time like this. "Sorry. Force of habit. But think about it," he said. "Seriously. If you'd known what was to come, would you have lived the way you have?"

May shook her pretty head and tiptoed over to the water's edge. "I don't believe it," she said, stamping a tiny tarsus. "I won't believe it."

"Denial is the first stage," Old Dan said. "It's quite natural."

"But it isn't fair," said Manny. "It isn't right." His terminal filaments twitched with agitation. "If we'd known at the start that we'd have only just this one day, we might have . . ."

"What?" said Old Dan. "You might have what? Decided against emerging? Passed at your chance to taste some of that"—

he paused to nod in the direction of pretty May at the shoreline—"sweetness?" He rolled himself another sticky ball. "I don't think so," he said, gently.

May blushed, and Manny joined her at the shoreline. Their wings touched. "No, you're right," said Manny. "I wouldn't have missed this for the world."

"Remember," said May, "when we first rose to the surface in that bright bubble of air? When we first saw the sky? When we first saw each other?" She caught the rainbow glimmer of a trout in the corner of her farthest eye and nudged Manny, gently, out of harm's way. "Remember how the sun looked, and felt, on our tender exoskeletons during our first molt?"

Manny gazed at May's slender abdomen, her many lovely eyes. "I remember," he said. "I was still panting on that leaf—a dull, pubescent subimago, as I watched you transform before my very eyes, into the transparent beauty that you are." His wings seemed to cloud up all over again as he reminisced. "And then you flew away! I thought I'd never catch you!"

May's thorax pulsed. "But you did catch me, my darling. In mid-flight!" She cast a quick fond glance at both of Manny's penes. "I was in absolute heaven," she said.

"But we might not get another chance," said Manny. He looked accusingly at Old Dan. His anger was returning.

"Good. Very good," said Old Dan. "Anger is the second stage. Not healthy to keep it inside." He was just rounding off the edges of his fourth brown ball. "Sorry. Can't help myself," he said. "It's what I do."

"But I don't understand," said Manny, in a weakening voice. His exoskeleton was already losing its sheen. "Why were we gifted with this consciousness, if our bodies were destined to be so temporary?" He climbed over a small, smooth pebble. "It's a cruel joke is what it is."

Old Dan shook his pronotum. "It is a mystery," he said. "But if it's any comfort, you two are the only ones who have this gift." He climbed up on one of his dung balls then and rested his aching femurs. "Look at them," he said, indicating the millions of mayflies who were just then clotting in the sky. "Most of them will end up on a windshield somewhere. Or piled up in drifts on some porch, or heaped in a doorway. They will fly mindlessly, thoughtlessly, as they have for billions of years. None of them have your gifts."

"Darling?" said May. Manny's color was fading fast. He could no longer stand. May caressed him with her filaments, with her antennae, with her vestigial mouthparts. "My dearest love!"

Then she looked at Old Dan squarely. "Gifts? You mean curses, don't you?" Her voice was crackling with bitterness. "Why should we know about our future if we haven't the power to change it?" She watched Manny's filaments soften. "He is dying already, isn't he."

Old Dan nodded.

"Then I defy you, stars!" May said, shaking a tiny tibia at the heavens. She trembled then, and walked in circles. "But surely there is something I can do to help him? Breathe life into him for a little while longer? What if I do good deeds? What if I fly up there right now and warn my sisters and brothers? What if I can get them to rise up with me to fight our terrible Fate?"

"Pretty May," said Old Dan. "There's no bargaining with Fate. We each have our job in the world. Consider, for a moment. If you could really choose to live another creature's life, would you? Think about it. Which would you prefer: To live a long, scarabbed, protected life eating, breathing, rolling dung? Or to live an ephemeral but shimmering life filled with flight, lovemaking, procreation?"

But May had stopped listening. She was huddled at Manny's side, losing some of her shimmer herself. "Do not go gently into that good night," she whispered.

Manny stirred, flicked one of his terminal filaments. "When I have fears that I may cease to be . . ."

"Shhhh," said May. "Don't tire yourself. I'm here beside you." To Old Dan she said, "It seems like just this morning that we met, and loved, and . . ."

"It was," said Old Dan.

". . . and I will go next, won't I."

He nodded. "If you have laid your eggs."

"I have." She lay down beside Manny then, closed some of her eyes. And she would never see her babies either. She thought of them, bright nymphs already, and already moving toward their own breathless flights and loves and shimmering sorrows. She'd keep that sadness to herself.

Manny's words were quiet as the moonlight. "And when I feel, fair creature of an hour, that I shall never look upon thee more . . ."

"Look upon me now," said May. "I'm coming with you. O, speak again, Bright Angel!"

Old Dan watched them, sadly. "Shit," he said, when it happened. He'd known it was coming—again—but that never made death any easier. Always a shocker, no matter how prepared you think you are. Always a kick in the gut. And it had been his fate to outlive hundreds of generations of his glittering mayfly friends. It had been his fate, also, to impart to a select few the hardest type of wisdom. And May and Manny had not, in fact, been the only ones to be gifted with an understanding of their own mortality—that was a lie he'd told to flatter them in their final minutes. There'd been others, scores of others. And each time Old Dan had wrestled again with his dung-covered self, debating the complex pros and cons of whether or not to forewarn them of their futures. And each time, ultimately, painful knowledge had triumphed over blissful ignorance. Rightly.

He rolled his perfectly round dung balls proudly, one by one, to encircle their faded, splintering corpses. "Merde," he said kindly, in lieu of a blessing. Then he left them in peace and went back to his work. He'd done all a dung beetle could do.

The Education of Old Dan

Old Dan hadn't always been old. He'd started out as a tender larva, just like everyone else, but was fortunate enough to have been born into a family that went back over forty million years—as his uncle kept all the time reminding him.

"We're Minotaurs!" Uncle Gordon often proclaimed. "None of that Dor blood in our veins." Uncle Gordon was a master roller, and took almost as much pride in his abilities as he did in his lineage. "More than likely we are direct descendants of Ra himself."

Young Dan understood early on that he was meant to ask, "Who's Ra?" whenever the subject came up. But that was purely a courtesy and a gesture of respect. No self-respecting dung beetle would be ignorant of that answer.

"Ra?" Uncle Gordon would pretend to be appalled that his own nephew—no, more a son than a nephew, ever since the day he took little Danny under his own epipleural fold when his dear sister and her husband, bless their souls, found themselves on the wrong side of that gigantic boot—would *not* know who Ra was! "Why, Ra was only the sacred sun god of ancient Egypt! He was the beginning!" And Uncle Gordon was just beginning then too, Dan knew. "He rolled his divine dung ball east to west—just like the sun—the source of all existence!" Uncle Gordon sometimes got so wrapped up in his explaining, that he'd squish the very dung ball he was shaping. "Crap," he'd say at times like that, though he warned Dan sternly against taking the name of The Source in vain.

Uncle Gordon provided young Dan with a lively, but respectable upbringing. He warned him against the evils of hanging out with carrion beetles (they chewed up dead shrews to make their nests, and then regurgitated those same nests to feed their larvae!) and threatened to disown his nephew completely if he *ever* saw him messing around those nasty little thieves who stole dung and eggs from their own kind. "Kleptoparasites," said Uncle Gordon, "are the *absolute lowest* form of scarabaeidae."

So, with the help of Uncle Gordon, Dan grew into a healthy and responsible young male. He worked hard, was burlier than most of his peers, and soon prided himself on being able to move fifty times his own weight in dung. This show of strength was not lost on the young females and they began to roll small balls in his direction, just to see what he would do. He liked the attention— wouldn't you? And he liked his job, and he liked being of Minotaur stock, and he began to feel fairly smug about his corner of the world and about his enviable place within it.

Until one day, while going after some very attractive sheep dung (his personal favorite) in the meadow, he chanced upon a spray of yellow fennel. And though he was not partial to the flowers themselves—that odor!—his eyes fell on something so colorful on the petals that he stopped in his muddy tracks to get a closer look. There, on the yellow fennel, was a fine family of tumbling flower beetles, sunning themselves.

He felt shyness for the first time. He felt, suddenly, the coarseness of his dark, dung-covered cuticle, the spininess of his tibial claws, the clumsiness of his blocky thorax. Their coats were striated with white, yellow, red. Their torsos were delicate, their necks defined. He scuttled under the fennel bush to hide himself, but as he did, he accidentally bumped against its stem and twelve little tumbling flower beetles tumbled onto the ferny foliage.

Dan apologized, tried to back away, was beside himself with embarrassment.

The tumbled beetles grumbled a bit, but seeing that Dan meant them no harm, climbed back up onto their sunny fennel.

All except one. She studied Dan, and refused to move. "You're very dirty," she observed, but not unkindly.

His tarsi were paralyzed; he couldn't have scurried away if he'd wanted to. He gazed at the downy yellow suns that adorned her back. Her brightness was a wonder—it almost hurt to look at her. But he couldn't look away, not even when he felt himself staring, rude, coarse beyond belief. "And you," he said, finally, "are the loveliest creature I've ever seen."

She laughed, but not unkindly.

What to do? What to say? She was so close, and he was so . . . he looked around for something to give her, some offering of friendship to show her that he . . . and there, just three kemklots away, was the shiny round ball of sheep dung he'd been rolling. "Wait here," he said. He scuttled toward it, and in a fever of excitement, nudged it back—though in his hurry he misjudged the requisite pressure needed to keep it at once rolling and intact. By the time he reached her, it was crumbling and misshapen—not at all his best work.

But she understood his intentions and was careful—miracle that she was of good breeding and compassion—to regard it as the most wonderful gift she'd ever received.

"Try some," he said, nudging it closer.

But here she declined, politely, and perhaps a little sadly. "But I eat only nectar," she said, by way of apology.

Her father called down from the fennel. "Persie!" he said, sharply. "We're waiting for you!"

"Persie," Dan said, savoring the sound of her name—its weight, density, texture.

"Persephone," she corrected him, as she turned to climb back up the fennel. She paused. "Will I see you again?"

His heart leapt, his claws quivered. Yes! he said, yes! you will, yes! And he watched her ascend, up through the ferny foliage, up the tall stalk, up into the slender branches, up onto the delicate yellow flowers. When she reached her family, she gazed back down on him and he saw himself as she must have seen him: dark and dirty and skulking in the underworld. "Can you fly?" he called up, but she didn't hear him.

All that day and the next, Dan moped around. Uncle Gordon indulged him for a while, but then he grew impatient. "What's eating you?" he said. But Dan couldn't answer. He'd lost his appetite for everything, even the choicest dung that Uncle Gordon had set aside, for family only, in the small larder of their underground home.

"Am I dirty?" Dan finally asked him.

Uncle Gordon eyed him warily. "Who has been filling your head with that shit?"

"I met someone," said Dan. "She was bright, and clean, and lived in the sun."

Uncle Gordon turned away. He was chewing on his own memories, apparently. Dan half expected him to blow up, curse the sun and everything under it. But he didn't. He didn't even speak, in fact, for a very long time. "Forget about her," he said only.

"But I . . ."

"Trust me on this."

And Dan did trust him, always had. But this was something that even Uncle Gordon couldn't understand. This was Love.

"Get back to work," said Uncle Gordon. "Work's the only remedy."

So he had. He tried. He rolled balls and balls of dung. Big balls, bigger balls, faster, faster. He skipped meals and tunneled and rolled, tunneled and rolled. When the females came by he flirted—gave it all he had. He accepted their small balls and he piled them into ostentatious shapes and structures. "Well, I declare," one of them said, "that is the biggest thing I've ever seen!" And he accepted all compliments and tried to let them feed his soul, but he came to understand that their words, their stares, their admiration, fed only his ego. Nothing more. And try as he might, his soul just kept shriveling. His soul he had left in a sunny field of fennel, on the bright yellow back of a tumbling flower beetle.

So he sought out the sun, and he thought of his love. And he conjured up ways to find her, to take her—to steal her if he had to—to bring her back with him to his underground home.

"Forget it," said Uncle Gordon one evening, as if reading his mind. "It's been done before. That kind of love kills."

And Dan knew he was right. She needed the sun. She needed her nectars. She needed so much more than he ever could give her. So Dan spent long minutes gazing at the sun, hoping that the rays themselves would connect them, would relay to her his words: But I, being poor, have only my dreams. I have spread my dreams under your feet. Tread softly, because you tread on my dreams.

His work suffered. Dan felt himself drained by the sun and by his longing for Persephone. He stopped rolling dung balls. Gradually at first, but then altogether.

"You need a vacation," Uncle Gordon told him. "Get away for a while."

So Dan took himself away from the dung balls, away from the hungry glances of the females. He took himself to the top of a hill and then he opened up his hard elytra, let his wings emerge. They were still good, strong wings, though he hadn't exercised them for a while. A stiff breeze lifted him, and he was off.

The world looked different from up high. He saw his friends below as insignificant black shapes who spent their days moving larger black shapes, but for what? to what end? They rolled dung, buried dung, laid their eggs inside of dung, but why? So those eggs could eat dung and grow strong? So they could then roll dung, bury dung, lay new eggs inside of dung to be born, to eat, to grow . . . and so it went, for ever and ever. Why even live? he wondered then. Why even work?

He flew farther and saw green forests, blue water, endless sky. What lay beyond that hill, he wondered, or that one? The colors were dazzling—reds, purples, oranges, yellows—ah, the yellows again. His heart had been lifting, but once more it fell into the memory of her downy yellow back, her tapering abdomen, her lovely and delicate neck. He sunk lower and lower in the sky.

Then all at once he was surrounded! Winged creatures were everywhere, buzzing and fluttering and battling for space. He felt her before he saw her—her graceful bearing, her fennel scent—

Persephone! He ducked and dodged her many brothers and sisters, aunts, uncles, cousins, until at last—beside her.

"Oh," she said. Her eyes softened. "I've been thinking about you. I couldn't help myself. I didn't know if I'd ever see you again."

He couldn't speak. It was all he could do to keep airborne—he'd been flying for such a long time already and the sight of her weakened him. "Can we get somewhere," he whispered, "by ourselves?"

She nodded and led him to a patch of unoccupied sky. They hovered in silence a moment, each savoring the proximity of the other.

"What should we do?" she said at last. Her despair weighed visibly on her wings.

"What can we do?" he said, though he was imagining them right then, right there, intertwined and spinning, writhing, whipping the very clouds into a froth with their passion. He felt his maleness rising.

"After all," she said, her voice sullied with contempt, "it's not as if we're common mayflies."

"What do you mean?" He was losing altitude.

"Oh, you know," she said, dipping with him in the sky. "They're not like us. No one thinks a thing if they . . . you know . . . in front of everyone . . ."

"Love each other?" The earth was getting closer and he hadn't the strength to ascend again. It was as if she'd pithed him right in the scutellum. He pulled away, and saw her with new eyes. She was an elitist. Worse. A bigot.

"What is it, Dan? You look different."

The real world came rushing up. "Some woman's yellow hair has maddened every mother's son." Disappointment made him careless with his words.

She was sinking too. They were nearly at ground level. She looked at him quizzically, then sorrowfully, and then with some annoyance.

"Yeats," he said. "Now I must wither into the truth."

"Wither away," she called back as she tumbled into a bed of blooming dill. "Go back to your dung heap."

He would. He did. And when he told Uncle Gordon what had happened, his uncle listened carefully. Then he led Dan outside, told him to wake up and smell the manure. "Look around you," he said. "The whole world lays at your coxa." And, as if on cue, three sturdy, lusty females rolled to Dan some fresh, new, mini-balls of dung. "Secret of happiness?" said Uncle Gordon. "Get yourself a good digger."

Old Dan was always glad that he had heeded his uncle's words. He'd found himself a shapely, cheerful digger who worked hard, laid lots of eggs, and who wasn't above inviting their many friends—may-flies included—into their cool and dung-filled dwelling.

But now and then, when the sun fell soft on a spray of yellow flowers, he thought of Persephone's yellow hair, and permitted himself a sweet, fennel-scented moment of regret, for all that never was and that would never, ever, be.

Fireflies of the Vanities

Another opening. Another show. You leave 'em laughing and there you go. Crystal and Dick approached the night with unexamined resignation, the same way they approached everything else. Allegra, in preparation for her Art, turned her energies inward; Fanny was already dancing in the bushes; Blake preened luxuriously, though somewhat petulantly, at the still pond; Spicy couldn't wait to bare it all again; Guy was in it just for tail; and Rosalee, dull and splotchy Rosalee, was seeing it as the means that could, this time perhaps, lead to bigger and better ends. Only Blue remained subdued. And this was a conscious choice on his part. Too many nights had he raced to join the magic that might save him. Only to be disappointed. Too many nights.

"Blue" was not his real name, but it was what the others called him. Something had always been a little off in his bioluminescence—instead of glowing the brilliant yellow of his compadres, his abdominal segments lit up in a murky blue that looked awfully like the night sky itself. But his parents had been supportive. The entire Lampyridae family, as a matter of fact, had been careful and kind about his congenital disorder. And for a long time that was enough. For a long time, his friends sought him out because he told funny jokes, like the one about how many Hercules beetles it took to screw in an artifact of artificial luminescence, or the one about what you call a dwarf spider without legs. Or they sought him out because he knew stuff that they didn't, like about how there were some fireflies in faraway lands that could flash in synchronized patterns, or about how some humans did nothing all day but tap buttons on boxes to make black marks appear on white surfaces.

But all too soon, Blue and his friends grew up and began to need more than sophomoric jokes and crazy stories. In truth, Blue himself had been the first to tire of his own inane prattle, even before his friends' attentions began wandering to affairs of the heart. Affairs of the genitalia, to be more accurate. Blue had been the only one, it seemed, who still honored the mysteries of the heart.

In the buzzings of the hot, July nights, more and more he fantasized about finding his own true love. Someone to fly beside, sleep beside, wake beside. And unlike the others, Blue was open-minded; he could look past the brightness, the speed, the perfectly proportioned segments, that the others required. He was looking for something much deeper and more important.

So he joined the others in the warm, Vermont sky, dancing wildly, passionately, flashing his dim blue bulb for all it was worth, praying that some worthy, intelligent female would see him for what he really was—smart, funny, loving, romantic—and not be blinded by a superficial display of meaningless glitz. And more and more, he'd found himself alone, bereft, humiliated in front of all of his family and friends, in front of even the growing human audience that came to the edge of the meadow to watch.

Guy urged Blue on, and Blue appreciated it, and he didn't want to harbor petty thoughts, but he couldn't help observing nonetheless that Guy's terminalia seemed to be the brightest part about him. "Turn it up, Dawg!" Guy said, every time he passed Blue in the muggy sky. Females flew to Guy in swarms. Blue couldn't understand it. He considered asking Guy for his secret, but "Turn it up, Dawg" comprised the bulk of Guy's vocabulary and it was hard to respect a bug like that.

Even Blake got more than his share of females, and this was particularly irksome to Blue because Blake didn't even like females.

It was widely known, though never spoken, that Blake would have cheerfully forgone any female attachments at all if the curse of his own exceptional beauty and his heightened sense of duty hadn't kept him always at their mercy. "I know they can't help themselves," he confided to Blue once. "I'd want me too," he said, with just the tiniest touch of irony. "But what about what *I* want?" Blake studied the slender stem of a maple leaf instead of meeting Blue's gaze. It was an uncharacteristically self-pitying moment that made Blue uneasy. "Never mind," Blake said. "You just don't get it."

But Blue did get it. At least he thought he did. He knew what it felt like to long for something always out of reach. "It must be very hard for you," Blue said.

"Que sera sera." Then Blake leapt up and shook off his sadness. He sparkled mischievously. "Witches can be right. Giants can be good. You decide what's right. You decide what's good."

Blue swallowed his annoyance. So like Blake to "say it with Sondheim." It was a quirk that many, Blue included, found a bit tiresome. Blake was a good friend though. He'd been one of Blue's earliest defenders. He'd once chased off a swarm of neighboring fireflies who'd lured Blue into their circle and then laughed at the deficiencies of his glow. "Being close and being clever's not like being true," he told Blue. And then, ever reluctant to abandon a song mid-phrase he added, "I don't need to, I would never, hide a thing from you . . . like sommme."

Blue watched Allegra warming up. She was a puzzlement to Blue; she prepared for her nightly performance with the single-minded concentration of a bug on its way to the zapper. And she'd always been that way—too busy crafting her performance to play with the others, always flexing, stretching, practicing her movements, choreographing even the patterns of her flashings. She meditated before each upsurgence and then usually flew off by herself. "Look at that one," the human watchers often said, in wonder at her artistry. She was the real thing, was Allegra, and Blue admired both her talent and her integrity, even if she never did give Blue a second glance.

Spicy was something else again. Like Allegra, she also prepared for the nightly performance, but her goals had nothing to do with

Art. She was an exhibitionist, pure and simple. She'd been born with exceptionally curvaceous segments and she liked nothing better than to shake them in front of any bug who'd pay attention. She never hovered demurely beneath the leaves either, as did so many females, waiting for a signal from a male. No, sir. Nothing demure about Spicy, thought Blue, and her vivacity might have been attractive if it weren't for the craven meanness with which she treated any male who actually fell for her flashy tease.

Blue might have a chance with Fanny. She was all light and joy and sensuality. Not too choosy either. She seemed to embrace any fellow flier, male or female, with the same easy familiarity with which she embraced the night. "I LOVE to fly," she often said. "I LOVE to shine!" It was endearing at first, almost infectious. For a while, Blue had seen in Fanny his ticket out of the lonely and bitter land he found himself more and more inhabiting. "Of course," she gushed, when he asked her for a turn. "You're one of my oldest and dearest friends!" But it was little more than a pity coupling, Blue saw. Love was out of the question.

"What do you think about Rosalee?" Blue asked Blake one hot afternoon that was all too quickly lengthening into yet another interminable summer night.

Blake cocked his handsome pronotum. "Someone is on your side. Someone else is not."

"What does that mean?"

Blake took a long time to answer. "Rosalee wants only what is good for Rosalee," he said. "Be careful."

Blue took offense, partly because he was getting desperate for some good news, but mainly because he feared that Blake was probably right. "You just don't want me to be happy."

Blake moved to comfort him.

"Get away from me," said Blue. "I'm not one of your buggering bugs." And then, because he felt so ashamed of himself already, he added, "And I'm sick of Sondheim too, so don't even start."

Just then a group of nubile females came wriggling by. Blake turned his head away. Not like him, thought Blue. What was he hiding?

"All I'm saying," Blue overheard Spicy say, "is that I wouldn't want a boyfriend who was prettier than me."

"Me neither," said Blake, just loud enough for Blue to hear.

That night, Blue decided to join Allegra up in her corner of the sky. He'd be invisible there, eclipsed by her light and her talent. "Do you mind?" he asked her.

She continued her pirouettes, as choreographed, before she answered. "If you were anyone else, I might," she said. "But you, Blue?" she undulated her luminous abdominal segment, slowly at first, then faster and faster, building to a dramatic climax. "You're a good bug, Blue. I don't mind you here at all."

He felt like he'd just been knighted by a queen. He gradually relaxed, and then he tried to copy some of her movements, mimicking her dips and flutters and antenna-sweeps. He felt strangely secure in his attempts since no one could see him anyway.

"Pretty good!" Allegra said. She was kinder than he'd thought. "Try this," she said, expertly demonstrating a slow-motion rolling triple abdominal curl.

He tried. Failed miserably. They both laughed.

"Not bad, though," she said. "You're braver than the rest of them."

Blue felt his pronotum pinkening. "And you're nicer," said Blue.

Allegra stopped laughing and hid her glowing abdomen behind a leaf. "You know, Blue. I have to tell you. You're a dying breed."

He rested on a branch beside her. It was hard to keep flying once the sad thoughts crept in. "I know. I am."

She surprised him by moving in closer. "And I am too. Artists don't last long in a world like ours."

Blue nodded. He hadn't thought of that before. "So, what should we do?"

Allegra leapt off the branch and began spinning in the sky. "As for me," she said, spacing out her words so one flew to him with each rotation, "I'll—just—dance—it—fills—me." She propelled herself with her strong, diligently trained tarsi, up higher, higher, then dove back down to his level. "But you, Blue. I worry. You need someone."

"What do you think about Rosalee?" He heard the eagerness in his voice and was instantly ashamed.

Allegra hovered in mid-air; her light pulsed like a heartbeat. "Demons will charm you with a smile, for a while, but in time . . ."

Blue laughed. "Oh, no! You sound like Blake."

She smiled. "Exactly." She took tiny little *jeté* leaps away from him as she spoke. "Blake."

"What do you mean?" he called after her. But Blue was glad she'd left; their conversation was going nowhere. Blake. Allegra. Both so full of themselves and both so wrong. Blue knew what he needed, and it wasn't an artist or a nancy bug either. It was Rosalee. Dull, splotchy little Rosalee. He congratulated himself on being able to see beyond her imperfections. He'd seek her out. He would. He didn't care what anyone said. Didn't he deserve a little happiness too?

Blue found her near a sugar maple, hovering demurely beneath the branches just as any good, self-respecting female should be. She was surprised to see him. She said he was too late. That she was already fading for the night.

He found her reticence, indeed, her very fatigue, appealing. "I'll never pressure you," Blue said. "I'm in this for the long haul."

Rosalee looked confused.

"I think you're lovely," Blue pressed on. "No matter what anyone says. I always have."

Rosalee rubbed one splotched tarsi against another. She was interested, clearly. "But what will you give me?"

Now Blue was confused. What, exactly, was she asking? She didn't appear to be as grateful for his attentions as he'd anticipated. "Love?" he said. "Happiness? Eggs? Isn't that enough?"

"But your segment won't even light." Her voice had gone cold. "And besides that, you're too . . ." she appeared to be searching the veins of a leaf for the words.

"Too what? What am I too . . . ?" he demanded.

She was wracking her tiny brain—he could see that—but then she had it, the very word. "Judgmental," she said. "I could never be with someone who was always looking and judging, like you do."

"But I'd never . . ."

"You know you would," she said. "You are right now." She pushed off into the sky without another word.

He let her go.

Blue hid his dim blue light in the bushes. From his hiding place he could watch the dazzling show in the soft, dark sky. So exquisitely beautiful. Why couldn't he be a part of all that? He saw his parents and siblings and cousins and friends. He saw Crystal and Dick going at it mechanically, as always. He saw Guy in hot pursuit of Spicy and thought that that would serve them both just about right. He saw Fanny, joyous Fanny, coupling with every leaf and bug that brushed along her sensuous abdomen. He saw Allegra in the starlight and heard the appreciative ahhhs of the human watchers at the edge of the ridge. He saw Rosalee batting her dull and splotchy antennae at scores of males, but holding out for her rewards. Rosalee was right, Rosalee was smarter than she looked; Blue *was* judgmental. And mean, sometimes. And stupid sometimes, too.

Blue saw Blake high above him then, brilliant and brave. Dutifully servicing females for the good of the species. Dutifully populating the skies with other beautiful, brave, brilliant little Blakes. Blake to the rescue. Blake at his side. Good, kind Blake—handsome inside and out. Blue didn't deserve him, but there he was, right there above him.

"Isn't it rich," Blue sang softly. "Aren't we a pair? I'm here at last on the ground—you're in mid-air." Blake couldn't hear him. Blue would have to fly up there and sing it louder. Closer. And soon. And for the rest of his life. What a fool he'd been. Blake and Blue. That sounded familiar, somehow. Right. It was all suddenly so perfectly clear. And then he couldn't wait to tell him—not another minute. Corny and true—that was Blake. Just exactly what Blue needed. He would fly up and tell him—then, right then—without judgment, without pride—and the dark sky opened up as Allegra flashed her approval—and hope for forgiveness.

To Kill a Katydid

You push off into the sky. The camellias are sticky with the wrong smell and your wings dip down, falter, fail. You just make it to the glass. Firm and warm. Safe. Here you can stretch your femurs. Rest. Try not to breathe too deeply.

You see them, moving in from the other side of the glass—huge, curious, bending creatures. They are peering at your undersides. Rudely, yes, but can you blame them? Clearly, they're transfixed. They exercise their mandibles and emit low, fluctuating vibra-tions. The way you stick your tarsi to the glass, then peeeeel them off again. Enchanting. It *is* quite a trick and not every katydid can do it correctly. They love you. They want more, and why shouldn't you indulge them? Poor things have so little in their lives to amuse them. Very well, then. You can give them that much.

You begin by clicking together your mandibles. That always pulls them in. Next, you draw your long and lovely tibia through the sharpened edges. You chew on your tarsi—for effect, mostly—the creatures back away, then move in closer—but also because your tarsi need cleaning. It's a dirty world, and this window, as a matter of record, might be more conscientiously maintained. But there you go again. You and your outdated values—*Victorian,* your brother called them. But is it so awful to care about cleanliness?

To take pride in yourself, in your surroundings? To *work,* for pity's sake? To do some work of noble note before you shuffle off this mortal coil?

Focus, you tell yourself. You're here now. And you have an appreciative audience. You rub your front tibia over your face. They go wild. So you do it once more. And then once again. Your wits are still a bit befuddled from that shower of poison, truth be known. But it wasn't their fault. They thought they were killing something bad.

You forgive them. Katydids are, by nature, a forgiving lot. You want them to know this. So you rub your face three more times. Amazing grace! How dismal must be the lives of these creatures that one clichéd move could evoke such delight? But you're getting weary now—you cannot, indeed, hold up the world. Show's over. Almost. For your *pièce de résistance,* you take hold of one long and lovely antennae with your tibia, and then you smooth it, groom it, through your mandibles. You have always considered your graceful antennae to be your best feature and you are pleased that they seem to agree. You savor this last delicious spattering of adulation. You know these creatures to have limited attention spans. Soon they will drift away into their own burrows or nests to do whatever it is that fills their days. But not quite yet! You flick your antennae flamboyantly—a cheap trick, but effective—they hold fast to their posts. And you are just about to show them how your jointed body can bend to caress the second antennae, when they see it. Your missing leg. No duh, you want to say. Took you long enough. But you really wish they hadn't noticed. Look at my antennae! You want to shout it. You can bend it double, then pull it out, bit by bit. Loop de loo, you show them. Watch this. Too late. They are fixated now on your missing limb. You know what comes next. First the horror. Then the pity. Then the turning away.

Always the same. Though to be fair, these creatures lingered a little longer than did your own brother before turning away. "Invalid," Rey said when he saw it. "What happened?" his wife inquired, more politely. You started to explain, about the large, whiskered, sand colored creature who . . . "Makes no difference," Rey cut in. "Tenny's disabled now. Totally useless."

Useless? You were hardly some sooty Dickensian cripple. "I beg your pardon," you said, affecting precisely the tone of voice that you knew Rey abhorred.

"Beg whatever you want," Rey said. "You'll need the practice." Then he rubbed his own back legs against his wings. Just like him to stridulate in the face of your misfortune. But he did sing beautifully and, in spite of her disapproval, his wife was drawn to his side. "See?" Rey said. "No song, no mate."

You knew this already. No song, no mate. And your singing days were over. As were your jumping days, for joy or otherwise. But the worst part would be the loneliness. It hadn't quite hit yet, but you knew it was coming. As Rey did. He'd always mocked your fastidiousness, and dismissed your limited athleticism, but he knew—he did know—that you shared with him an abiding and inexhaustible love for females. No song, no mate. It hadn't needed saying. Of course Rey would be a prick. But you could still fly. There was that. You flew at Rey's head and clubbed him with your front tarsi. He laughed, ducked away. "Don't look for any handouts here," Rey said then. You wanted to tell him where he might shove his handouts, but you didn't. Disabled or not, you would not stoop.

You faced the meadow alone. The grasses were higher than you'd remembered. And worse, they were teeming with Conocephalinae. Not just with Gracillimus, like yourself, but with the Spartinae, Robustus, Monstrosa orders as well. The Diabolica you feared most of all. So you were surprised when Creetin, one particularly intimidating and territorial Diabolica, honored you with something approaching sympathy. "That's gotta suck," he said, jerking his chiseled pronotum at your missing limb.

You were grateful for the kindness. Perhaps, in another world, Creetin might have been a friend. But you clicked your wings, tersely, in acknowledgement. You knew that any other response might be interpreted as weakness. They had their own codes, those Diabolicas. So you limped on by, trying hard not to limp, knowing that he was undoubtedly still watching and that any evidence of self-pity might trigger his attack response. Still, once safely out of eyeshot, you let your guard down and wept, just a little, because he was right about it sucking. It really did.

As did the mud that you found yourself suddenly mired in. Who would have thought that one leg could matter so much? You'd never realized before how much leverage it provided in sticky situations. Always, you had prided yourself on your light-footedness, on your lithe and lively movements. You were a Gracillimus, after all, the most graceful of the meadow katydids. "On, Dancer!" your friends had chanted, in happier times. But now.

A brown beetle passed on your right without even a nod. He was one of those sturdy, common, single-minded specimens for whom polite small talk is an effort. And besides, he was intent on his task—rolling a large, round clump of mud—let's hope it was mud—out of the meadow. To where? Who knows where, but he left you behind without even a nod, and the mud—you really hope it was only mud—clung to your remaining legs, and the more you pushed against it, the deeper it sucked you down. Betrayal, you thought. Your own body. You permitted yourself one long self-indulgent moment of despair. So. Was this to be the end of your short and handsome life? Trapped, un-mourned, in the muck—friendless, songless, filthy—and besides that, almost wholly un-actualized?

To your credit, you did not give in to that swampy sadness. You rallied, rather, in one super-orthopterian effort, to lift yourself out of that stupidly sticky predicament. I will die one day, you told yourself, but it won't be here and it won't be like this. And it wasn't, and you did, somehow—lift yourself—up into the reeds. And as you basked there in the sun, breathing hard, feeling grateful and victimized, and just a little bit arrogant, all at once, you reassessed priorities—to be, or not to be—that was the question. And when you settled on the former, finally, purely, determinedly, the reeds parted before you and you saw all the way into the future. Adventure, yes! However crippled and crabbed might be your gait, it would take you to the edges of the meadow, to the edges of the world. *To strive, to seek, to find, and not to yield.* And there you would begin.

But it had taken you first to a crowd of bush crickets, singing.

"Melodious!" you said, having recognized the song of their order.

They paused when you spoke.

"Don't stop," you told them. "I love that song. I used to sing it with my sisters—on fall afternoons as we leapt on orange leaves and exulted in those . . ."

They glared at you.

"wheels of weeds, long and lovely and lush." Good old Hopkins. You loved him almost as much as you did Tennyson, your namesake. For all their faults, those Victorians were just more substantive than the Romantics. They were just more, well, manly. "Mind if I join you?"

Apparently they did. One very green cricket shoved his way forward and clicked right in your face. His mother chastised him. "No need to be rude," she said. "Just ignore him and he'll go away."

She was right. Unacknowledged lives would simply disappear. "Crickets," you muttered. You congratulated yourself that whatever else you might have lost, that at least you still had your pride. To lose *that* would be fatal indeed. You used to feel sorry for crickets, but then, well, just then you felt that perhaps they deserved the humiliation of being clothed, in the human public's imagination, in those silly little shoes with spats and those ridiculous tuxedos. You pressed on. "See ya in the funny papers," you said, as sardonically as you could manage, before you limped away.

Humiliation. The irony would have been delectable had it not tasted so bitterly of truth. Because—if you were really honest with yourself—you had to acknowledge that it had been you, your own self, who had been humiliated. By them, by Rey, by that ignorant bewhiskered creature who'd consumed your identity with one flick of his sandpapery tongue. And now, even now, by the very humans who'd been applauding your achievements just moments before.

Fate. That most ruthless of predators. And which course required the most courage? Acceptance? Or shaking one's tarsi defiantly at God?

You slide down the glass and try to hide your deformity. Acceptance. You will not flaunt your disability, will not use it to coerce some wobbly-minded human into fussing and fawning over your poor, pathetic little handicapped self, into setting you up in one of those pink cardboard structures with holes in the lid and limp leaves to nibble. That would be the ultimate debasement. Worse even than this—disabled in the prime of life, and huddled beneath a discarded pile of dead roses. *I fall upon the thorns of life! I bleed!*

Dear God. Pull yourself together. You may be low, but quoting a *Romantic—?*

You wrack your brain for better words on which to build your future, however short it may be. *Break, break, break, on thy gray stones.* No, not that one. *I will drink life to the lees.* Better. You can focus on that for a while, and stretch out your remaining legs and try, once more, to create a little music. For a moment, you think it works. *Zeet, zip, zip,* you hear, with all the old sweetness. But it is just the wind, singing in the branches above you. Dignity, you remind yourself. These decomposing roses are strangely erotic. Damn. One less vanity. You limp into a strange, hard corner. The surface is rough and cold. It has no give. So. This is how it's going to end. Without even the comfort of a close, warm earth to bury yourself inside. You cover your inadequacies with a curling leaf. The fumes of the old poison hang still and heavy in the darkening air. A ribbon of fireflies pulse in the distance. You dare not breathe. *Death closes all.* But what might yet be done?

A sharp light bursts against the evening. The heavy glass slides open. "Buggy!" a small voice says. You cringe. You fold yourself more neatly beneath the thorns and leaves. Perhaps she will not think to look here. Or perhaps she'll be put off by those wicked looking thorns. *Buggy?* Please no.

"Where are you, little buggy?"

You pray that she will just go ahead and step on you with her padded pedipalps and put you out of your misery.

She lifts up the leaves and nearly impales you on a sharp thorn. "Oh!" says the nectar-laden voice. "There you are, little buggy!"

You plead with God to spare you this. Haven't you suffered enough? Haven't you faced all His trials with dignity and courage? Why this . . . defilement at the end of all your sorrows? The human hand caresses your antennae. In her mindless love, she scrapes your abdomen into the concrete and snaps another tibia. *Are God and Nature then at strife?* You long for the clarity of Rey's contempt, for the purity of the crickets' scorn. Either would be preferable to this descent into helplessness. Fate? You search your memory for anything that might give your last moments some worth.

Freeeeeeedommmmmm! you shout, inwardly. You imagine crowds cheering.

You are dangled, then dropped, into her pretty pink box. You hope for that final flash of illumination before the end. For always roaming with a hungry heart, much have I seen and known. Limp leaves surround you. A thorny stem has been provided for your comfort. Now more than ever seems it rich to die. No, please— no Romantic submission. Free will. Yes. Thank you, Alfred Lord. Courage. Action. The cardboard lid is lowered, fastened. Small specks of life, bright moons, can still be glimpsed through the holes she punctured. You must hurry—there may yet be enough poison in the air. You forgive your brother for his disabling arrogance; you forgive this child for the handicap of youth; you forgive the world for its blind, deaf, crippling ignorance. Then you inhale. Deeply, deliberately. As though to breathe were life. You strive. You seek. You find. You do not yield. You do not ever yield. You follow knowledge like a sinking star.

Mantis Prayers

Gabriel heard voices, and noises, and occasionally music. He saw things sometimes too. But mostly he just heard their words and wondered, why are they speaking to me?

He'd traveled that morning to the edge of the pond to watch the orange sun rise and to lap cool dew off blades of grass. Perfect silence. A Mourning Cloak rested above him, on the edge of a tree stump. Gabriel bowed his head in deference. There was one butterfly he would never dream of harming, not even if the higher laws had not forbidden it. "Go in peace," he told the butterfly as it pumped its wings and then rose into the air. Gabriel took a long, restful moment to savor the sanctity and the blessed quiet of the pond.

It wore a mantis down sometimes—all those voices, bright and dark. All those jangled souls clamoring to be heard. And as much as he loved to climb up the rocky arches of the headstones and snatch midges from inside the deep-etched crevasses of their inscriptions, even Gabriel needed a break now and then from the ghosts in the graveyard.

Sweet mercy. And here was a living voice in the natural world. The song of a katydid calling to his mate. Gabriel watched the katydid's lazy, languid movements in the tall grass. He swayed himself to the easy rhythms, leaned in to hear its song more clearly—admirably ardent!—then caught it in his spiny forelegs, chomped down on its neck and had himself some breakfast. Gabriel wondered, as he ate, why the voices told him all their troubles when there was really nothing he could do.

But the voices gave his days a purpose and a shape, and he felt, in truth, a certain responsibility. To sit on the headstones and to hear all their stories. To be the designated keeper of their histories. It was a charming life, mainly. He could see the entire castle from his headstone vantage. And the duck pond. And the fluttering fennel. And the rolling green meadows and the fluffs of white sheep.

He missed it already—too quiet by the pond—he'd make his way back. There were bridges to traverse, fences to crawl under, hedges of sharp-thorned roses to thread himself through. But he loved the challenges—the very epicness—of the journey. He drew strength from a present so electrified with pasts.

The damp earth of the graveyard cushioned his tarsi when he returned. Rain, rain, every day rain. And it was beautiful, yes, life-giving, but tiresome too, and sometimes it drowned out the voices. And today, after his nourishing respite, he felt full and happy and anxious to hear them again. "Speak," Gabriel said as he climbed up his favorite headstone, stepping over fresh midges (the katydid had left him surprisingly satiated) and "Ready," he said, when he reached the top. Then he closed his ocelli to the light and reverently folded his tibia in front of his triangular pronotum.

Gabriel heard just a lot of static at first—the indistinguishable shouts and rough laughter of a rabble, a squeaky wagon on cobblestones, the lowing of a cow—but that was to be expected. It took a few minutes for the frequencies to settle and for the real voices to begin.

Music today. Opera! Wagner, if he wasn't mistaken. The voices were singing in words he couldn't understand, but the melody was dark, throbbing—unexpectedly stirring. He wished, as he often did, for a female partner to share with him the mysteries of this graveyard and of this castle. Of course he'd heard that ugly rumor about females decapitating their mates, but he'd never quite believed it. Perhaps certain females might take the upper hand with more delicately constituted mates, but Gabriel was a powerful male—rather strikingly so, he thought when he caught his reflection in a puddle—and no female was ever going to bite off *his* head, thank you very much. Still, he supposed that one couldn't be too careful. And besides, he was somewhat set in his solitary ways. Probably wiser, and kinder too in the long run, to remain a bachelor and to savor the opera alone.

The singing trailed off into a final sob. A female voice spoke: *I longed for an opera passion. . . .* This was a new voice. Gabriel listened more intently . . . *with spitless kisses. All angled shadows and high planed cheekbones.* Gabriel straightened on his perch; he was rather vain of his raptorial good looks and she did seem to be describing someone very like himself in her soliloquy, poor woman. *I longed for a raw-boned man on a tall black horse. His mission would be urgent, but he would stop for me. He'd lean down from his tall steed to kiss me sternly, purely, with closed, dry lips and tragic eyes. And I, for my part, would lift my face to him and* (static again) . . . *but my father . . .* the voice broke off there, began to weep. So often the case, thought Gabriel. Another unrequited love. Too bad. Better to have loved and lost . . . and all that, he suspected. But he didn't really know. He'd been given many gifts, he reminded himself, but knowing love had not been one of them.

He heard swords clashing then, the clank of steel on armor. An adventure! Heavy man-grunts and shoves. A good deal of savage swearing. The odor of onions and tinny metal. A sharp, slicing sound when sword met flesh. A groan. A final curse. And then, silence. Gabriel bowed his head respectfully. But wait. Not over yet. A young girl's cry, the slosh of water. A man's anguished voice: *Leave me! I'm meant to die here!* The sound of an earthen bowl being scraped across the floor, ripping garments, cloths rung out in water, moans, soft and sorry. *Hush* (the girl)—*I'll not let you die.* Heavy footsteps—the other man's return. An unsheathing of a sword. The girl's scream. *No!* (the first man.) *Watch!* (the second.) More screams and scuffling, moaning, clanking. The girl's strangled, blood-gurgling cry. The sword across her white throat,

Gabriel suspected. Then a gallop of horses. *Let me die too,* the first man said to the girl. But he hadn't died then, Gabriel knew. Because then the man got to his feet, lifted the girl—cradled her nearly severed head when it fell backwards—and stood before Gabriel in the graveyard.

Gabriel was trembling. His own leafy coat had changed to the ashy color of the headstone. *Cheated!* the man's voice cried out again—his must have been the voice that called to Gabriel sometimes in the middle of the night. It was sad, sad, unbearably sad. *I was the one meant to die,* the man said. *Why was it I who kept living?*

Gabriel closed four of his eyes, kept his tibia crossed before him. He felt as if he were supposed to have the answer. But he didn't. The ghost disappeared.

An old woman's quavery voice broke in: *My darlings? Where are you, my angels?* Gabriel had heard this voice before too. Something had happened to her children, Gabriel surmised from fragments of earlier visitations. The speaker appeared before him then, in the shimmering sunshine, transparent as a mayfly. She showed herself to Gabriel as a young woman, raven-haired, with an infant in her arms. *You'll not have him,* she said, to some unseen adversary. The old woman had been quite lovely in her youth, Gabriel decided. Elegant and slender, with a finely chiseled, triangular head—a nearly perfect specimen. Spirited. He liked that in a female. Gabriel felt the opera stirrings again.

Then, as if to throw a cold shower on his wandering thoughts, another, shriller voice said, *Give him to me! You made your choice!* A shattering of crystal, an infant's wail. *Take him to the window,* the speaker commanded. Heavy boots on a carpet. Gabriel looked up at the castle. Oh. That window. He'd seen it hundreds of times across the meadow. High, narrow, crooked. Cut deep into an eastern turret. Gabriel saw it all again—the infant caught in the grip of two black leather gloves, its baptismal gown dangling from that crooked window; the raven-haired beauty pleading for her child, clawing for him, screaming, *Please God my son!* The leather gloves opening.

Oh. The suffering these creatures endured. Gabriel had never known anything like it and prayed he never would. Still, he felt the weight of their sorrows press on him like loose floor stones in the chapel. He bowed his head. "God?" he said when the sun warmed his ocelli. No answer. He hadn't really expected one. But why was God so silent when His creations were so noisy? Gabriel gazed down at the weed-choked grave beneath him; immediately, the sky began to tighten and a light rain fell through the still-glowing sun. Fine droplets pooled in the sodden earth. He started to descend but stopped, looked again. The world was upside down! The sun lay beneath him, reflected in the sheen of shallow water.

So many miracles in one lifetime.

A tiny water strider had already discovered the puddle. Hardly worth the effort, thought Gabriel, but a snack might be prudent. Very well then, though he knew he needn't hurry. Striders were so single minded; they never thought to look up. Plenty of time yet to savor these fine, brooding clouds before he climbed down for his nourishment.

The darkening clouds oozed over the sky, shape-shifting as they traveled. Gabriel sighed. These were the times when he most yearned for a soul-mate. But one made of real cuticle and blood— not one of those sorrowing shades. To have a living soul to gaze with him at the bright beetles by day, at the flitting fireflies by night; to reflect with him on the limits of the universe and on their place within it. He succumbed, for a moment, to a self-indulgent melancholy. To know that kind of companionship would be very close to paradise indeed.

Gabriel was beginning to feel a bit lightheaded. He really should climb down—those crows with their cawings, with their beaks close together, were making him nervous. Not that they were any match for a mantis. They hadn't any foresight, for one thing. No instinct for strategy whatsoever. Nevertheless, there were six of them and one of him and perhaps it was time to take cover, with dignity, before they decided to get those foul-smelling beaks any closer.

But before Gabriel could so much as clench his maxillae he felt something lifting him up, up off the headstone, up past the castle turrets, up past the very treetops. He felt helpless, outside of himself, but strangely calm, as if he were watching it all happen to someone else. "God?" No answer.

No pain either. No paralysis. No panic. He looked around, cautiously. He was not at all sure what kind of a device was keeping him aloft, but since his wits—and nary a crow claw—were about him and since he kept on rising higher, higher, he eventually ascended into an understanding that this was, in very truth, some kind of a bonafide *miracle,* and he saw himself sailing over the duck pond, the green meadow, again, again. But he didn't fall. He couldn't fall. *Something* would not let him fall.

He saw the earth as a soft, green lily pad, suddenly very dear and very far away. He felt a humming about him, as if thousands of thousands of insect wings were beating all at once. "God?" he said again, to the thrumming air. No answer, just ecstatic vibrations, as if thousands of thousands of tiny antennae were happily palpitating and caressing his exoskeleton at the same time. A perfect peace flowed in through his esophagus, wound around his tracheal tubes, and flew out again from his spiracles. He had never felt so wholly alive. The world below him was filled with creatures, large and small. They all—humans and ghosts, elephants and aphids—seemed to him, suddenly, of equal worth and stature. His compound eyes saw everything at once, from every angle, stereoscopically. God was everywhere.

Gabriel watched with new compassion the strugglings of the tiny strider he had only moments before regarded as lunch. He saw the strider's very soul in his own expanded consciousness. Never again would he regard the rumblings of his own stomach as being more important than the needs of his fellow creatures. Never again would he witness the suffering of others without taking steps to ameliorate it.

Perhaps, thought Gabriel, God had chosen him for some special task. Perhaps he was an angel already! Perhaps, and this thought filled Gabriel with so much self-righteousness that he began to sink under the weight of it, Gabriel was actually of a higher order than were all the other species on earth and God had lifted him up to the heavens to show him.

He floated down, down, through the vast Ethereal Skie, sailing between worlds and worlds, winnowing the buxom Air. At last he descended into the castle garden lightly, gracefully, and with a majesty, thought Gabriel, that befitted his new station on earth. *Paradise Lost,* thought Gabriel. It was walled on three sides and Gabriel looked with wonder on the abundance of colors and perfumes and shady retreats. He would settle here, he decided, and wait for a sign. He wandered up and around a vine of morning glories, savoring the divinity of its essence, and resisting a disturbingly powerful impulse to skewer a honey bee that was just then probing for nectar with its long proboscis.

"Bless your spirit, honeybee," Gabriel said, with some effort. He was beginning to feel the rumblings of hunger again and to impale a fat honeybee had always (previous to the miracle) been one of life's sweetest pleasures. This was going to be harder than he thought. He hoped the sign would come soon. He hunkered down beneath some squash flowers and prayed for guidance.

And then, as if in answer, Gabriel watched as a male honeybee buzzed down beside the female and, with no discernible foreplay or sweet talk whatsoever, mounted her. Gabriel felt the opera stirrings again, along with a sharp stab of regret. Was it his Fate, then, to complete his lifecycle alone? Perhaps, as an angel, he was meant to remain a virgin. He thanked God for this new wisdom, but kept one of his eyes open, just in case. He saw then a sight that made his ganglia shrivel. The mating apparatus of the male exploded inside the female and came unhooked from his body. Fool for Love! thought Gabriel. But then he thought again. About the perfect harmony of their lovemaking. About the interdependencies of all God's creatures—the cruelties with the kindnesses. About one's roles and purposes in this life and how best to fulfill one's potentials.

And as he pondered these unfathomable mysteries, the scent of something familiar but unfamiliar, longed for but dreaded, sailed to him on a breeze. "God?" But when he saw her he said, "Ah. God's gift."

She was beautiful—all angled shadows and high planed cheek-bones in the twilight. She eyed him warily, stood her ground. "Husband?" she said.

He nearly wept. God's plan for him unfolded like the wings of the Mourning Cloak that just then fluttered above their heads.

"I'm hungry," said his beautiful Destiny.

"Me too." And then he told her of his miraculous experience in the sky, and of the spirits that gifted him with their voices. He grew rapturous as he spoke. Here at last he'd found his helpmeet, to comfort him in his sorrows and to work beside him in his ministrations to the needy. "I will always provide for you, my love. God has given us our choice of creatures to sustain us. We need only to respect His gifts, and honor them with our compassion." And though it scarcely needed saying, he added, "But we may never touch the Mourning Cloak." He indicated, with a jerk of his pronotum, the higher laws of the heavens. "That, as you must know, is forbidden."

She was silent. She appeared to understand. She swayed seductively in the tender evening. Theirs would be a truly blessed union. But then, just as Gabriel was looking down, checking anxiously to see if his hindlegs were appropriately groomed, she struck at the air, caught the gold-fringed wings of the Mourning Cloak mid-flight, in the barbs of her tibia. She clasped the juicy thorax in her strong mandible. "Be innocent of the knowledge," she whispered sweetly, "though thou wilst applaud the deed."

Gabriel stood before her, paralyzed with horror.

Night fell then, and swiftly. What to do. What to do. All darkness and no hope. They would be banished from Paradise. Shamed forever. "What's done cannot be undone," she said, as if in answer to his thoughts. But her figure in the moonlight was irresistible; the opera voices suddenly hurled themselves into the garden—the soaring sopranos, the boom of the baritones—all thrumming, beating, throbbing passion. They sang to Gabriel of ecstasies, of tragedies, of love, of life, of death. Gabriel gazed long at her lovely silhouette, more perfect than a spider's web at dawn. She would bring him to completion; she would bring him to his doom. She swayed again, seductively. She moved in closer.

And then Gabriel felt his body plunging, exploding, ecstatically torn. At last. Consummation. "Give him to me," an opera voice rang out. "I'll save him!" a second voice sang. From what? Gabriel felt himself rising again, separated from his body as before, but this time in the misty starless night, and this time in a different, bloodier way. And then all the voices of the graveyard were everywhere around him, intertwining themselves into the arias and oratorios, holding him safe, cradling his severed head, weeping and whispering in hushed tones, with reverence, fear, anger, panic.

Then they all fell silent. They touched each other's faces, with just their shadowy and trembling fingertips. "At least he wasn't cheated," said a low, ragged male voice. "At least he'll be with us now," whispered a weary female. But they wept together, nonetheless. Some of them sobbed. No one now to hear them. No one left to listen. They turned on Gabriel's mate. "You did this," they told her. "You ruined everything."

But she had just cracked into Gabriel's exoskeleton and was slurping out his juices, and between the crunch of his chitin and the click click of her own mandibles, she never heard a thing.

Trouble in Thebes:
A Butterfly Tragedy

CAST OF CHARACTERS, IN ORDER OF APPEARANCE:

Ed Rex, the king: Monarch
Terence, the blind seer: Gray Pansy
Jackie, Ed's wife: Mourning Cloak
Creon (The Neon), Ed's brother-in-law: Great Spangled Fritillary

PROLOGUE:
> When the cat asked the riddle, Ed was ready.
> "Groovy," said Sphinxy. Then she ate her own tail and all
> the twigs and mice that were stuck to it. She swallowed her
> voice along with a seriously awesome hairball.
> "Guess you won't be messing with my homies after this," Ed
> said to the now-silent feline.

TERENCE:
> *Flicking his antennae.* Yeah. Think I heard that story about,
> I don't know, *ten thousand* times already. You bad. Okay?

ED:

> Just take a look at these guns. *He stretches out his enormous orange and black wings, then waves them at Terence's compound eyes.*

TERENCE:

> You know I can't see them. I'm *blind*, remember?

ED:

> So what? You can feel them, can't you? Feel all that air these big beauties push around. *He pumps his wings repeatedly, making Terence's antennae flutter.*

TERENCE:

> Yeah. They're big, okay? You bad. I already said. Can we talk about something important now?

ED:

> Like what?

TERENCE:

> Like the fact that all your "homies" are falling down dead again.

ED:

> You got it all wrong, Terry. I fixed that little problem. With the riddle, remember?

TERENCE:

> Yeah, but that was then and this is now. And there's no crazy cat behind it this time.

MOTH CHORUS:

> No crazy cat! Now our afflictions have no end!
> See, how our lives like butterflies take wing

Though pallid caterpillars laden with death
Lie unwept in the stony ways,
For the day ravages what the night spares!

ED:

What's with all the moths? Don't they have some flame to go visit or something? *Pulls in his wings, looks suddenly deflated.* My homies are sick again?

TERENCE:

You got it.

ED:

Damn. That's harsh. What should I do?

TERENCE:

Ask him. *He indicates Creon "the Neon."*

CREON:

Hey, Butts. What's shakin'?

ED:

My subjects. *The black lines in his wings grow darker.* They're dying.

CREON:

Gee, ya think? Well that would account for all those carcasses out there. You don't get out much, do you Ed. Of course they're dying. Where you think I been all this time?

ED:

Where you think I think you been? Flittin' off, as usual—mackin' on some violets.

CREON:

> Hey, don't go dissin' my violets. At least they leave my breath sweet. Not like your—what is that you eat? Oh yeah. MILK weed. Makes you smell like crap—like you're one of them freakin' dung slingers. That's why no one—you may have noticed this—will come near you except this blind old geezer here.

ED:

> And Jackie! O! My Jackie!

CREON:

> Yeah, well. You're the king. The freakin' rex. She has to.

TERENCE:

> *Annoyed.* What a couple of stupid cocoons.

ED:

> Hey!

CREON:

> Hey!

TERENCE:

> Exactly.

Jackie floats down between them, looking sorrowful, but regal.

TERENCE:

> My lady.

JACKIE:

> Are they at it again?

TERENCE:

> Alas.

JACKIE:

> *Turning to her husband.* Ed?

ED:

> O! Jackie O!

JACKIE:

> Yes, Ed, it's me. Still me. *To Terence.* Makes me miss old Laios sometimes, bless his cranky old soul. *To Ed.* So, my handsome husband, what is the news?

ED:

> News, my love?

JACKIE:

> Yes. Me. Still here. News.

ED:

> *Stammering.* My subjects. Our subjects. They are . . . *He is momentarily distracted by the glistening gold trim of her wings.* Dying, O Jackie! *He is suddenly, earnestly distraught.* They are dying.

JACKIE:

> Dying? But why?

TERENCE:

> Another plague.

JACKIE:

> What is the cause?

TERENCE:

> Don't ask.

JACKIE:

> Why not?

TERENCE:

> Trust me on this.

ED:

> What kind of an answer is that? What are you hiding?

CREON:

> Get off his case, Ed. He's just an old pansy. He don't know jack. He's just jerkin your chain.

ED:

> Huh?

CREON:

> Fuhgettaboutit.

ED:

> Huh?

CREON:

> Pith me.

TERENCE:

> Gladly.

Creon flies away.

MOTH CHORUS:

> The song they sang when you came here to Thebes
> And found your misguided berthing.
> All this, and more, that you can not now guess,
> Will bring you to yourself, among your children.

ED:

Terence? Help a brother out here. I know I'm not the brightest monarch in the meadow, but I can see that something rank is going down. And that you know something you're not spilling. But I need to know. So I'm asking you again. I'm begging you. Please, Terence. I, the monarch, am begging you. And in front of my beautiful queen. Tell me, please. What should I do?

TERENCE:

Thoughtful, moved. My dear boy. I am sorry. But you've already done it.

ED:

Huh?

JACKIE:

Please don't start that again.

TERENCE:

I'll put it another way. *Pumps his old gray wings slowly, trying to find the words.* Sometimes, without meaning to, we make mistakes.

ED:

Like that time when you mistook Jackie—my Jackie—for your own wife? I remember that. It was dark, and . . .

TERENCE:

Yes, well, something like that, yes. Except that, of course, being blind and all, I can't be expected to always . . .

ED:

No big, T. I got it. You're blind. You couldn't see. Stuff happens. Mistakes.

TERENCE:

Yes, yes, exactly. Mistakes.

JACKIE:

Really Terry. If you know something, why don't you tell the boy? You can see how puffed up he's getting.

TERENCE:

Sadly. You don't know what you're asking.

JACKIE:

Cautiously. What do you mean? *I* don't know? What's all this to do with me?

TERENCE:

I will never tell you what I know! Now it is my misery; then, it would be yours!

JACKIE:

Is all the drama really necessary?

TERENCE:

Angrily. You doubt me?

JACKIE:

Why shouldn't I? You've been wrong before.

TERENCE:

I? Never!

JACKIE:

What about that time, when Laios and I were newly emerged. Remember what you told us then, about how . . .

TERENCE:

Don't go there, Jackie.

JACKIE:

But you said . . .

ED:

What did he say?

TERENCE:

Nothing. Another riddle.

ED:

A riddle? Excellent! I love riddles. You might say I've a call-ing. Remember Sphinxy?

JACKIE:

It wasn't a riddle, dear. It was a prophecy. *Moves closer to Terence.* Wasn't it, Terence.

TERENCE:

Yes. *He tries to fly away, but his wings are suddenly weak.*

JACKIE:

Looking at Terence, but speaking to Ed. Fortunately, proph-ecies are even lamer than riddles. It made no sense at all. Stuff about "a blind monarch who has eyes now. A penni-less monarch, who is rich now." *She sees something in Ter-ence's blind eyes that frightens her.*

TERENCE:

Go on then, since you've started.

ED:

You're right. It makes no sense at all. But go on, since you've started. You look so ravishing in the moonlight. What else was in the prophecy?

JACKIE:

> *Losing her color. She recites mechanically now, remembering every word.* "To the children with whom he lives now he will be brother and father—the very same. To her who bore him, son and husband—the very same."

TERENCE:

> Jackie.

ED:

> But how can that be? Makes no sense at all.

TERENCE:

> Jackie, you couldn't have known.

JACKIE:

> "Who came to his father's bed, wet with his father's blood."

TERENCE:

> Hush, darling. Say no more.

ED:

> Darling? Where you get off calling my woman darling?

TERENCE:

> Bewildered as a blown bird, my soul hovers and cannot find foothold.

ED:

> Huh?

TERENCE:

> Don't leave us, Jackie. Not like this.

JACKIE:

> *Whirling on him.* How would you have me leave you?

ED:

Leave? Who's leaving? What? Why?

MOTH CHORUS:

For wisdom changes hands among the wise.
Alas for the seed of monarchs.
Your splendor is all fallen.
The greatest griefs are those we cause ourselves.

ED:

What? Who are these stupid moths anyway? And why do
they keep interrupting? Away, away, I say! Not you, Jackie.
O Jackie! Never you! Why are you leaving? Why do you
leave me?

JACKIE:

Alas for the seed of monarchs. *She goes to Ed and brushes a
dark wing against his quivering antennae.* You still don't get
it, do you Eddie? Merciful meadow! May you never learn
who you are. *She flies away.*

ED:

Who I am?

TERENCE:

"Child by Laios doomed to die, then doomed to lose that
fortunate little death."

ED:

What?

TERENCE:

For God's sake, Ed! How dense are you? You are the one
who caused this plague. That's why all your homies are dy-

ing. Because of you. Because of the nastiness you brought to Thebes. It's all because of you, Ed! You!

ED:

Me?

TERENCE:

Muttering to himself and walking in circles. Chorus of moths? Help me out here, would you?

MOTH CHORUS:

Ah, the net of incest, mingling fathers, brothers, sons, with brides, wives, mothers: the last evil that can be known— How evil!

ED:

Laughing. Evil? Me?

TERENCE:

Enraged. What is wrong with you? Why can't you get it? You've got to get it. Or this can't be a proper tragedy. The tragic hero has got to have his moment of recognition! Geez.

ED:

Take a chill pill, T. I get it. Damned in my birth, in my marriage bed, damned. I get it, okay? It sucks to be me.

TERENCE:

But you're not upset? You're not going to gouge out your own eyes or exile yourself or anything?

ED:

Don't think I can do that, T. Sorry.

TERENCE:

>But what about the catharsis! How are we ever going to end this thing without a proper catharsis!

ED:

>What's this catharsis stuff? I don't need no stinkin' catharsis.

TERENCE:

>But the audience does, Ed. That's what they came to get.

ED:

>Audience? What's an audience?

TERENCE:

>Onlookers, eavesdroppers, readers . . . whatever you want to call them. And they need a tragedy. A real tragedy. One with suspense—unbearable suspense. And with a reversal, recognition, an angst-relieving catharsis—the whole ball of pollen.

ED:

>*His antennae twitch spasmodically as he nervously looks around.* Where are they? Are they here now? Are they watching us?

TERENCE:

>Always. There is always an audience.

ED:

>Always?

TERENCE:

>Always. And a script too. For each one of us.

ED:

> A script? You're freakin' me out, man. What's a script?

TERENCE:

> The words we say. The thoughts we think. And everything we do. It's all scripted. It's Fate.

ED:

> But what if I improvise? What if I fly up in this tree instead of sitting on this bush? What if I decide to give up milkweed entirely—go out and find me some lilac or some other shit to eat—upset the whole order of the universe?

TERENCE:

> Then that would be what you'd been scripted to do. Sorry. There's no getting around Fate.

ED:

> *Draws in his wings and sits silently, motionless, for a long moment.* So what you're saying is that I've got to take the fall for some heinous crimes I didn't know I was committing, just for the sake of the eavesdroppers? To make *them* feel better?

TERENCE:

> Well, something like that . . .

ED:

> Just to make *them* feel as if their sad little lives aren't so bad after all?

TERENCE:

> Well, sort of. It's the whole pity and fear thing . . .

ED:

> Pity? You want them to pity me?

TERENCE:

> Yes! You've got it now. But don't take it so hard. They only pity you because they care—because you are such an admirable monarch.

ED:

> So if I'd been some cruel, ugly, unfeeling assassin bug . . .

TERENCE:

> No pity. No fear either—that's the beauty part. To be a real tragedy, they need to identify strongly enough with the protagonist, to feel genuine fear that it could happen to them.

ED:

> Because they don't identify with ugly bugs. They all want to see themselves as handsome monarchs. Something like that?

TERENCE:

> Well, yes, but . . .

ED:

> And then they want that handsome monarch to suffer, terribly, so they can suffer vicariously, just a little, and then go home to their pretty wives.

TERENCE:

> You've got it, Ed! Praise the gods!

ED:

> What gods?

TERENCE:

> The gods—you know. The gods who write the scripts and make everything happen the way it does.

ED:

> You're scaring me, T. You all of a sudden getting religious on me?

TERENCE:

> Well, there have to be gods.

ED:

> For butterflies? *He unfurls his wings again—they are dazzlingly orange.* Sounds to me like you're making an awfully dangerous assumption here. And you know what they say that "to assume" does to "U" and "ME".

TERENCE:

> Okay, okay. Let's forget about the gods for a minute, and . . .

ED:

> Forget about the gods? I'm moving away from you, bro—don't want to get zapped by lightning . . .

TERENCE:

> . . . and get back to the tragedy part. Come on, Ed. Be a sport. This has to be tragedy. That's why I'm here. I'm supposed to tell you what's going to happen.

ED:

> Knock yourself out, T. What *is* going to happen?

TERENCE:

> *Reanimated and energetic.* Well, first of all, you're going to be expecting someone to tell you that everything is just fine—that you didn't murder your father or sleep with your mother—that you didn't do anything wrong at all—but in the course of that conversation the opposite occurs—the *reversal,* it's called, and then right after that

you have your big *recognition*, which leads, of course, to your doing terrible, unspeakable things to yourself, which brings on the *catharsis*, yadda yadda, which we've already discussed, which allows everyone a good cry, and then they get to go home happy.

ED:

They go home happy? But what about my homies? The ones who dropped dead because of something I did in total ignorance? Do they spring up to life again?

TERENCE:

Well, no but . . .

ED:

And what about my wife/mother? Does she get to go home happy?

TERENCE:

Well, no. She suffers too—terribly, but . . .

ED:

And my kids? What happens to my kids?

TERENCE:

Well, they're cursed, of course. Forever. What else could they be?

ED:

And all because I have this *reversal/recognition* thing you're pushing me to have.

TERENCE:

Partly that, yes, but partly also that . . .

ED:

Well how bout *this* for a reversal: I REFUSE to accept the blame for something I did in innocence.

TERENCE:

But you can't refuse!

ED:

And then YOU have the recognition that I'm going to change the story and continue to live in blissful ignorance.

TERENCE:

But you can't do that. I'm not the tragic hero. It just doesn't work that way. *Turns to the chorus of moths—his wings twitching.* He can't do that, can he?

CHORUS:

Hmmmmmmmmmmmmmmmm
It is a mystery, a mystery!
But the story is already altered—the script already rewritten.
For it was you, old wise one, who was supposed to refuse
     the information,
He who was supposed to insist.
But you gave him the info without enough begging

So that's all gone to crap now.
          It is a mystery! Unfathomable!

ED:

Ha Ha!

CHORUS:

And the faintest flutter, it is said, of a butterfly's wings,
Is enough to change the world forever.

ED:

> *Flapping his wings forcefully.* Then change, world! Change!

TERENCE:

> Ah tomorrow and tomorrow and tomorrow! There would
> have been a time for such a word!

CHORUS:

> Wrong play, Terence.

TERENCE:

> My pronotum is spinning!

ED:

> *Still flapping his wings.* What else, Terence? What else was
> supposed to happen?

TERENCE:

> *Defeated, imploring the unseen audience, then turning back
> to Ed.* Not that it matters now, but, well, you would have
> come to an acceptance of your fate, eventually. But not un-
> til you had wandered the world in misery for a good long
> while, and been a burden on all who loved you.

ED:

> *Still flapping, though growing tired.* So you see! I just cut
> to the chase is all—saved everyone a lot of grief. It would
> have been hubris for me to have thought I was at fault for
> something Fate had planned for me, right?

TERENCE:

> Well, yes. *Brightening a bit.* And I am glad you used that
> word, *hubris. Gesturing toward the audience.* And they
> liked that too, but . . .

ED:

But nothing, bro. We're butterflies!

TERENCE:

But the tragedy! The audience! You've ruined the whole story.

ED:

Or I fixed it—for them and for us. *He climbs to the top of the milkweed bush and addresses all his subjects.* Rejoice! Rejoice! The plague is over! I recognized nothing! So we can all go on as we were!

TERENCE:

Fading and shrinking. I'm melting! I'm melting! What a world! What a world!

MOTH CHORUS:

Wrong story, T.
But Ed the Rex, what of your fallen subjects?
What of your mourning queen?

ED:

Bows his head in recognition. The black lines come back into his wings. We will grieve for the dead, of course. We will grieve together and we'll keep them always in our hearts. We owe them that, and will not forget. But then we'll return to the living. We will find a way to heal our ailing friends. We'll discover a new weed or we'll develop immunities or something. We always have. And then we'll fly again. We're butterflies.

TERENCE:

> *Perking up.* You may have something there, Ed. Perhaps I could use my legendary premonitory powers to come up with cures or something?

ED:

> Now you're talking!

TERENCE:

> And I suppose . . . It wouldn't kill anyone to just be happy for a minute, would it?

JACKIE:

> *Floating down again, visibly brighter. She speaks to the audience.* What a concept! You'd all be okay with a little bit of happiness, wouldn't you? *She moves upstage, whispers to the audience seductively.* I could make it worth your while.

ED:

> O! Wise and beauteous one!

CREON THE NEON:

> *Returns, flies to the very front of the stage, peers into the audience.* What up?

ED:

> Reality check, that's what. We're *butterflies!* How bad can things be? We fly, we eat, we copulate. We're devastatingly attractive.

CREON THE NEON:

> You got *that* right, brother. I'm pickin' up what you're puttin' down.

ED:

> And lookie here. I scored us some fine smooooth milk-weed, too. *Offers some to the audience.* Come on. Cheer up. Let's call this thing a "lite" tragedy—all the taste, but less filling and only half the calories! Huh? Huh? Whatcha think, huh?

JACKIE:

> *Cozies up beside Ed, accepts some of the milkweed.* Thank god for that wingspan.

The Unbearable Lightness of Bee-ing

Honey had it all. She'd been blessed with a fine pair of large and shapely wings; a long and agile proboscis through which to extract the deepest, sweetest nectar; an enviable sheen of soft, golden fuzz; and the gift of a shimmering buzz that soothed the other workers even as it stimulated the more recalcitrant drones for their stud-duties to the queen.

But something was not right. It was happening again. No, not now. Not again. Honey flew up, up, into the bright sunbeams to outrun the darkness. "Go away," she said, but it wouldn't, she knew. And there was nothing she could do about it either, not once it had blanketed her wings with its nets of heavy sorrow and had wedged its thick and sticky grayness between herself and the happy business of a bee's bright day. So often it appeared when she least expected it, too—in the middle of a waggle dance, in the middle of a pollen bath, in the middle of her buzzing song—and no matter how fast, how hard, how desperately she beat her wings and drank in the cheer of the vast blue sky, it just kept right on coming.

The other workers didn't understand. "Buck up, Hon," said Beatrice, when Honey finally confided in her that she felt, sometimes, like giving up. Beatrice was sucking down some nectar as she listened. "But how can you think that, Hon? When life is so sweet?"

Honey watched her friend's crop expand, bigger, bigger. It was just about to burst. "Be careful there, Bea."

Beatrice laughed. "I know my limitations." But she slowed down some, just the same. "So," she said, resting finally on a sturdy yellow petal. "So what is it, exactly, that's bugging you, girlfriend? It's heavy, you say? And gray?"

Honey nodded, and sank down onto a splintering fence post. "It's nothing," she told Beatrice. What else could she say? It was just . . . so hard to live sometimes.

"Imagine what it's like carrying around something like *this* every live-long day," said Beatrice, as she thrust out her distended abdomen. She was trying to be funny, Honey knew. Doing her best to be a good friend. But that only made Honey feel sadder and more guilty—to see her friend trying so hard, humiliating herself (and perhaps the entire hymenoptera order as well), just to cheer Honey up, and Honey too selfish to take her own sorry self out of her own selfish sadness long enough to let Beatrice think that she really had helped.

"You're right," said Honey, willing brightness into her ocelli, and forcefully flicking her antennae in a way meant to show light-heartedness. "I have nothing to be sad about." She dove deep into the heart of a peony and sucked back enough nectar to make her own crop bulge.

Suzanna buzzed over. "Whazzup?" she said, and before Honey could stop her, Beatrice—guileless Beatrice—laid Honey's dark secret right out there in the open.

"It's nothing, Suzanna." Honey blushed pink beneath the gold. "I'm better now."

Suzanna sized her up. "You know," she said, "that's just what happened to Zuzu."

Honey wished more than anything that Beatrice hadn't told Suzanna. She knew she was trying to help, but Suzanna? Suzanna plunged into gossip was like it was pollen, and then spread it around as fast as she could.

"Zuzu's wings never were very strong," Honey said, pumping her own. "And then with the wind, and that pool . . ." Honey shook her head. It was a sad enough memory without Suzanna trying to make it into something even worse.

"Bless her soul," said Beatrice.

Suzanna buzzed in short, ugly snorts. She looked around the meadow to see who might be listening. She moved in so close that Honey felt Suzanna's fuzz all bristled in her own. "Ssssssounds like . . ." she said, circling and savoring her news like a prize, ". . . ssssuicide."

"No way," said Beatrice. "She fell in, just like Honey said. And by the time that human scooped her out, it was too late."

"Silly, silly bees," said Suzanna. "Zuzu stung the human. Didn't you hear about that?"

Honey felt the darkness closing in. "That happens some-times—you know it does. The human touched her stinger. He did it to himself."

Just then, a band of disheartened looking drones passed over-head. Honey buzzed, sonorously, inspiringly, just for them. "Look up," she said. "They need our encouragement."

"Waste of space," said Suzanna, without acknowledging them at all.

"They can't help it," said Beatrice. "Poor things. Do you suppose they know, going in, that they're going to get ripped in half?" Sympathy flooded her compound eyes.

That was why you had to love Beatrice, even if she wasn't the brightest bee in the hive. She had a generous heart. She felt sorry for the drones instead of sneering at them, as Suzanna did. Honey really didn't like Suzanna, who was just then dusting herself with more pollen than any one bee had a right to. And she kept on bad-mouthing poor Zuzu besides.

Honey's sadness was giving way to anger. Good. Anger was easier. "You know that stingers can come loose," Honey said again. She wasn't about to let Suzanna have the last word on this. And how dare Suzanna say mean things about Zuzu—sweet and stoic Zuzu. "You know that can happen."

Suzanna sighed. "You silly, silly bees. You don't know what Zuzu told me, that very morning."

"What?" asked Beatrice, before Honey could stop her.

"That she felt like giving up, that's what." Suzanna let that sink in, before she turned her attentions again to her own triumphantly pollen-coated self.

Beatrice glanced at Honey, alarmed.

Honey felt the rosy color flaring up again. Stop looking at me! she wanted to say. The whole thing was just too stupid. She wouldn't stay.

"So, you really think," said Beatrice, quivering, "that Zuzu . . . killed herself?"

Suzanna didn't answer, just glared at Honey.

"But why would she?" asked Beatrice. "I mean, why would any bee . . ."

"I've got work to do," said Honey. "I'll see you at the hive." She took off into the terrifying twilight. "Depressssssed," she heard Suzanna buzz, before Honey was even out of range. Was she talking about Zuzu? Surely she wasn't talking about Honey. She better not be. Suzanna was pure mean. And wrong besides. Honey would work, work, work through this moment too. When she reached the hive—was it just her or was the hive a lot further away than it used to be?—she paused to help her youngest sisters fan the nectar. It was hard work, she remembered, but good training for the tasks that lay ahead for them. "Good job," she buzzed. "You are making us proud." The young workers flapped their wings harder in response.

Honey remembered those early days, when she was newly emerged and the world seemed so wide and bright and bursting with sweet possibilities. She couldn't wait, she remembered, to do her part for the hive. Honey had never been a lazy bee; she'd always found an inexplicable joy, in fact, in fashioning waxy combs with six perfect sides—no more, no less. And it gave her great pleasure to tend the young larvae—to feed and protect them, to clean out their cells, and to cap them off safely when they grew into pupae. She tended young workers and drones alike, and Honey prided herself on her ability to do so without making any sexist or judgmental distinctions between them. The drones *were* good for only one thing, it was true, and they *were* completely helpless, but they weren't really the spoiled gigolos that so many of the workers made them out to be. They paid for their brief moments of passion with their very lives, in fact. Or else they lived out their useless, idle, meaningless existences as virgins. It was very sad, really. Honey liked to think she played at least some small part in making their days more bearable.

And she liked to think also that she'd established herself, early on, as a bee one could trust. Not for Honey had there ever been any unseemly jostling for position, nor any ill will directed toward another. "Cooperation" was her buzz-word, and her peers, even the most cold-blooded among them, warmed in her presence and aired their petty rivalries elsewhere.

So Honey had generally been deeply contented with her lot, and always, in the past, had met adversity with courage and resiliency. But there, just then, on that warm summer night, the sadness clung to her bristly legs with the pollen and she couldn't—no matter how hard she tried—rake it off.

"Here you go, Sweetness," Honey whispered to a growing pupa as she sealed her in for her good, long rest. How many times had Honey laughingly said to her girlfriends that she'd certainly never want to go through that metamorphosis stage again. So boring! To just lie there and waste all that good flying time! And yet there she was, Honey realized, actually envying that pupa for being buried into that long, dark, quiet sleep.

"What's wrong with me?" said Honey. And she didn't realized that she had said it out loud until Beatrice buzzed up alongside her.

"There you are, Hon," said Beatrice. "I've been looking hither and thither for you. You need to slow down sometimes." She paused to give her own weary wings a rest from hauling around her growing plumpness. "You're gonna work yourself to death one of these days."

Honey pretended not to hear. She sealed in another pupa for her metamorphosis.

"You okay?" Beatrice said.

Honey nodded. No use in burdening friends with these ridiculous and unwarranted feelings. She was acting like a larva herself; she would shake it off and get her old self back. She tried to answer, but no words emerged. She was suddenly, unspeakably tired. Her buzz was gone.

"Hon?" said Beatrice, moving in closer. She was staring at Honey the way she had in the meadow.

"I'm perfect," said Honey. "Just a little tired, is all."

Beatrice studied the heavy load of pollen on Honey's third legs. "Well, there's your problem! Here," she said, busying herself with raking off the pollen with her own back leg combs, "let me help you with this." When she'd brushed off an impressive amount, she offered it back to Honey. "Eat this," she said. "Look at you! Pale as dust. Anybee can see that you need more protein." She dabbed out some honey from an unsealed cell and went to work on mixing it with the pollen. "Bee bread will fix you up, Hon, good as new. A bee can't live on nectar alone, you know."

Honey thanked her and accepted the mixture. Couldn't risk hurting her friend's feelings by refusing. And maybe Beatrice was right, besides. It had been a long time since Honey had ingested more than a few quick gulps of nectar—might be some chemical thing was all that was wrong with her—too many carbs and not enough protein.

"Get some rest," Beatrice said. She turned to go, then turned back again.

"I will," said Honey.

Still, Beatrice hovered. "Wind's coming up again. Be careful out there."

The next morning blew in fresh and new. Honey looked around her—nothing; pumped her wings—nothing; stretched her tarsi—nothing. A strange feeling—one she remembered, vaguely, like a happy dream—joy, freedom, elation—enveloped her. Had the darkness blown away in the night? Would it stay away for good? Honey tested her wings—light!—ah, to fly again! To really fly! Without the weight of the world beating her down.

The morning sunbeams danced on her antennae and she basked in their light. She was glad to the brink of fear.

"Wind, do your best," she said. "I am ready." She rolled in the breeze. So what happened? Had it really been just the bee bread that she needed? Rest? Of course it was. Food and rest. How silly she was to think herself above the basic bee necessities.

A swarm of drones passed, this time, beneath her. "Be brave!" she buzzed. "Be strong!" A mighty gust threatened to blow her into their midst, but she withstood it. That was close, she thought. I'd better be careful today, like Beatrice said. The world beneath her was wide and bright. She flew over the green clover, the yellow sunflowers, the blue pool. At the sight of the pool, memories of Zuzu threatened to blow her off course. Be brave, be strong! She righted herself. Good job. You can do it. She smiled inwardly as a bright family of tumbling flower beetles played in the fennel beneath her. They have no worries at all, she thought. How lovely that must be. Fly straight, she told herself. You have no worries either. You're not like Zuzu. You love your life.

And she did, she did, but the wind was strong and her strength was waning, and over there, just beyond that sweet grove of maples, she thought she saw the darkness sneaking in again.

Silly, silly bee, she told herself. It won't find you today. But just to be sure, she decided to dive down into the garden of gardenias. She'd hide from the wind and the darkness, both. She wouldn't be pulled into their traps. And while she was at it, she'd indulge herself in a little sweet gardenia nectar. Relax a minute. Listen to her body. No weakness in that, she told herself.

So Honey relaxed, and began her descent. But just as she did, the wind caught her again. She laughed at first, but when it wouldn't let go, when it carried her backwards, panic paralyzed her wings. The wind sucked her into its eddy then, and wouldn't let go. It spun her around and swept her back over the green clover, the yellow sunflowers. It swirled her, tarsi over antennae, into a maelstrom of sunflower heads and dandelion parachutes. Then, all that suddenly fell away.

Honey was over the pool. She watched the blue water rush up to meet her, and searched the heavens for a way out. Above her, darkness oozed across the horizon, stretched out its nets to catch her, fell over her wings. No. Not now. It couldn't happen now, not on this day when Honey had finally remembered how to live again. Not now, when she needed every bit of her strength to escape the reach of that blue water. Not now. She beat at it, buzzed at it, struggled to break through, escape back to the sweet blue sky, back to the morning when everything was new and good. There! She did it! She saw the blue and thought Sky! Freedom! Victory! And for a moment, all was still. The wind let go and she felt herself floating, resting, in a cloud of blue. Heaven? she wondered. She was light again—weightless—flying without even moving her wings—oh, ecstasy of effortless flight! But then she realized her mistake. Not sky. Water. A blue betrayal. Zuzu's pool.

Honey kicked and kicked. She tried to beat her wings but they wouldn't move. Had they fallen off? No, there they were, but they were laden with something. Despair? No. This something was glistening. Transparent. But it was also soaking into her fine golden fuzz, seeping into her proboscis, drowning out her shimmering buzz.

She kicked again. No help. She thought of all the lost moments of glimmering sunshine she had wasted in her battles against that treacherous darkness. She'd waged so many battles against it. And she'd almost won. This morning proved that she'd almost won. There was a comfort. She thought of Beatrice, of how sad she'd be when she heard about Honey's death. Then she thought about Suzanna. How she'd probably gloat. Spread rumors. Call it suicide, maybe. The thought of Suzanna made Honey struggle again. Please let me go, she said to the water. Please let me live, if only to redeem myself, and Zuzu. She kicked until her legs refused. Then she gave in. To the lightness, the peace, the floating peace, the sinking stillness. It's over then, she thought, with something like gratitude.

But it wasn't over. Something was lifting her, up into a breeze that chilled her, a sun that warmed her, and then there was something else—a smell, a feeling, a solidity and comfort that placed itself between Honey and the icy water. It was almost the color of honey. And it was warm. But it was solid, not sticky. She stretched her reviving legs against its small hills and valleys. Human, she realized. So this must be a human hand. She'd heard about them, but had never touched one before. And she heard a low murmur—a human buzz, she guessed—and even in her still-dizzy consciousness, she understood its kindness. It was trying to help. It was trying to save her.

Saved. Honey felt her spiracles drying, her air sac, her trachea. Saved. She thought of Beatrice, of the innocent pupae who would be waiting for her return.

Honey was going to live! Another chance. Was there anybee more in love with life than Honey at that very moment? Never! And the peace she had touched upon in that one sacred moment was not what she needed. It was life she needed. Life! With its smells, with its colors, with its work, and its trials. With its sweetness.

Honey made herself look away from the darkness pressing down on her again from the undersides of the sharp white clouds. She could fight it again. And again. She could do that. What was life without struggle, after all? She struggled for in instant in the human's hand, as if remembering. Preparing herself. And then, "Careful!" she told the human. "Do not flex your hand that way. Do not let it touch my stinger. Do not . . ."

The human buzz broke into a hard, angry sound; the hand flicked Honey from its safety. She hit the concrete, torn and empty, her stinger and entrails left behind. Over. Really over this time. Ironic, Honey thought, that her own defenses had destroyed her, after all the other forces had failed. She hoped that the human would not suffer too much for his good intentions. She hoped that Beatrice would not be too sad, that the pupae would be cared for and cherished. She hoped that death would be simply a new metamorphosis. But she hoped most of all, in those last slips of light, that she had not designed her own end.

Fly Paper

My thesis, I think, will be this: However loathsome and Filthy we seem to you, we are still Living beings, and as such, should not be condemned to this cruel and unusual torture for merely doing what we must to survive. Dantean is what it is—an outdated relic of a dead theology—but I am rambling now and must return to the classic Aristotelian Appeals if I am to have any hope of persuading anyone to my position. Supporting point #1 (Here's where I'll pull out the pathos): How would you like it if your food arrived on fEcal matter, or on discharges from open wounds, or on Sputum, spoiled eggs, rotten meat? How would you like to spend your days patrolling dumps and sewers and garbage heaps for your daily sustenance? How would you like it if regurgitation and excretion were the inevitable result of simply landing to rest? Or (the liberals in the bunch will nod empAthetically at this point and murmur about the inequity of it all): How would you feel if your human friends shooed you away every time you tried to enter into the conversation? I'll leave them saliVating on that for a while then move on to supporting point #2 (HEre's where I'm going to lay on the logos and stick in—ha, stick is a good word here—some quotes from authority):"Even though the order of Flies (Diptera) is much older, true houseflies are believed to have evolved in the beginning of the Cenozoic era, some 65 million years ago.[5] They are thought to have originated in the southern Palearctic region, particularly the MiddlE East. Because of their close, commensal relationship with man, they probably owe their worldwide dispersal to co-migration with humans."[3] Aha! Sounds smart, and proves that it's their fault that we're here at all! And besides that, it dignifies us with the title of "true houseflies" and once the concept of "truth" buzzes in, the intellectuals will start picking at each other like scabies. Supporting point #3: Somehow or other, I'm going to circle back to that Dante aLLusion in the intro to give the English majors something to savor. I will cite other examples from *The Inferno* (with its rivers of blood and deserts of flamiNG Sands) that show evidence of Dante's awesomely imaginative, if not overly merciful, vision. But then I'll twist it around—in a most impressive utilization of ethos—demonstrating that the main difference, however, between those sinners and us is that their punishments were *appropriate* to their sins, whereas THIS—this cruel and unusual entrapment, this slow death, this living hell, this sticky purgatory of dislOcated limbs and dreams deferred and futile strivings after freedom is entirely *inappropriate* to a crime consisting of trying only to nourish ourselves and our innOcent little maggots. Masticate on *that,* gentle readers. We are not heretics or traitors or hypocrites. Neither are we blasphemers, sodomites, panderers, or seducers. We're not even politicians. We cannot bite, as they do. We ingest only liquid food—what threat is there in that? We might—my own humbly oFfered suggestion—be made to lie in vile slush along with the gluttons, or be foRced, with the flatterers, to live stEEped in human excrement. Just an idea. But then I'll smack 'em with my conclusion: that it is *inhumane* for humans to treat us in this manner. Better to open the door and let us live out our Days in the fetid heat away from their precious slices of watermelon, better to hide their pastrami and let Time Itself reap its grim and grisly justice, better even to swat us with those flappity plastic things and put us out of our misery quickly, than to consign us to this sticky sheet where, Once stuck, well, then we're . . . you know what. I'll cry bias! Is it our appearance they object to? The hair-like projections that cover our body? The fact that we have only one pair of wings? Inadmissible evidence! Foul play! And then, once they are suitable chagrined, I'll call for the abolishMent of this outdated practice that does nothing to deter, after all, but speaks only to an unreasonable and uncivilized need for vengeance. And then I'll know real satisfaction at long last, having made my argument clearly and logically in one long sticky paragraph that I hope will fester like a sore and then run and crust and sugar over like a syrupy sweet, and thus make Aristotle, as well as Langston, very proud. Viva La Paradiso!!!

Teleological Matters

"Why do we shrink up when we die?"

Vladimir sighed. How to answer this one? "Just hold on," he whispered. "I'll explain it when we're alone."

"And why are we called 'Striders?' We don't stride. We don't even walk." Wylie studied the tiny ripples that fanned out behind him. "We kind of skate, actually. Kind of row."

Vlad had hoped that once, just this once, a threatening look might be enough to silence his inquisitive little brother. "I'm sorry," Vlad said to the grieving Mrs. Bitterman. "He doesn't mean any harm."

"Why is everyone so sad?" Wylie said. "Doesn't every one die?" He stopped asking questions long enough to consider again the tenuous surface of the water beneath his tarsi.

Mrs. Bitterman skated away slowly, her hair-fringed feet clearly weary of this life-long dance.

"Shekit," Vlad said to Wylie sharply. Wylie was getting too old for this kind of behavior. His constant questions had been cute when he was little, but he was getting bigger and one of their own had just perished. It was time for Wylie to start thinking about how others felt sometimes and . . .

"Why are we here?" Wylie asked.

Vlad nodded soberly to Mr. Slide and his son Seth, as they strode away. That meant the beautiful Nadia must be nearby too. She usually stayed pretty close to her father and brother—they insisted upon it, and Vlad couldn't blame them. Strider fights had been known to break out spontaneously when she passed—her very vibrations on the water were enough to fan male passions into violence. Vlad counted himself among the many foolish males who would die for her, though he hoped he had enough sense to know that fighting over Nadia was not the way to win her heart. She was finer than that. Deeper. He felt her slipping past him—wanted to stop her and to tell her of his love—of his fine, deep love for her—not superficial like the others, not lust alone, but real and lasting. He knew, however, this was neither the time nor the place. "We are here to pay our respects," he whispered to Wylie, trying to model for him the appropriate behavior.

Wylie laughed. "Not *here*," he said, indicating the tiny little patch of sad water where old Mr. Bitterman's shrunken corpse had floated into a tangle of weeds. "*Here*," he said, expansively, and by that Vlad understood him to mean here on this earth, here in this universe, cosmically, existentially here in the present.

"Because we *are*," Vlad said impatiently. He was watching Nadia skate away from him. "Stop asking questions. It's not all about you all the time."

"No," said Wylie, sulking. "It's all about *her*."

Vlad's anger flared, but he let the rest of the mourners pass before he responded. "Guess what, Wy. You don't know everything. You think you do, but you don't. So give it a rest, okay?"

Wylie looked chagrined. He scooted away and hovered near a lily pad.

Vlad felt his anger sink and his terror rise. "Don't hold still! You know what can happen!"

"I don't care," said Wylie.

"Well I do," said Vladimir, rushing to his side.

Wylie started skating again, halfheartedly. It took him a long time to speak and when he did, his voice was small and frightened. "Why did you get mad at me?"

"I'm sorry." He was. "I didn't mean to."

"Why did you then?"

Vlad sighed. "Because we can't always control our emotions."

"Why not?"

Vlad searched for the words—words he'd learned from Wylie himself—that might sound scientific enough to actually satisfy him for a while. "Because certain responses have been programmed into our collective unconsciousness and cannot be altered." He waited for the inevitable follow-up question. It didn't come. "You okay, Wy?"

Wylie nodded but Vlad could see that he was not. Vlad felt another stab in his collective unconscious. Poor little guy. He'd never known his parents, nor any of his siblings. He'd just appeared one day. A solitary nymph without a soul in the world to call his own. He'd latched onto Vladimir immediately. "Are you my brother?" were his first words.

Vladimir remembered that day so clearly. It was the day he'd told his first lie. "Yes," he'd said. "I am your brother, Vladimir."

"Vladimir. Vladimir." He'd skated around on his new little nymph legs and repeated Vlad's name, over and over. He was a thoughtful little guy. And smart too. Anyone could see that. "Vlad the Impaler!" he'd said suddenly, brightly.

"Vlad the who?"

"Impaler! Impaler! You're Vlad the Impaler!" He skated in tight, happy circles. "That's so cool," he said.

"I'm not an impaler," said Vlad. "I'm just a regular water bug."

"Otherwise known as a Jesus Bug."

"What?"

"You walk on water, don't you?"

"Same as you," Vlad said, but he was starting to suspect that they really weren't the same at all. This kid knew stuff. Weird stuff. He started to ask who the hell was this Jesus character anyway, but decided against it. "You walk on water too," Vlad said, stupidly. Almost accusingly.

"Yes," said the little fella, and he looked quite proud about that. "And you're an impaler." (Vlad was beginning to learn that his new little friend never let anything drop.) "We all are." He'd pointed to his mouthparts. "Why else would we have these rostrums?"

"Yeah. Right. Rostrums." Vlad remembered being awed by the kid. And a little bit frightened. This kid knew more than any self-respecting water strider had a right to. "You ask a lot of questions, don't you."

"Do I?"

"I think I'll call you 'Why'," Vlad said. For some crazy reason, he felt strangely elated around this peculiar little orphan nymph.

"That's not a real name." The little guy stopped skating then. Looked hurt.

"Sure it is," said Vlad quickly. (He was learning, too, just how fragile were his little friend's feelings.) "It's short for 'Wylie.'" Lie number two. "You were named for our father, Noah Wylie." Lie number three. Big lie. Why 'Noah'? Where did that come from? Lying was starting to come easy—that couldn't be right.

Vlad remembered that fateful day and felt ashamed again. Not about the lying—though perhaps he should feel worse about that than he did—but about losing his temper with poor little Wylie. "A good strider takes everything in stride," Vlad's own real father, Jonah—just plain Jonah—used to say. His real father had been very good, very wise. Vlad really wished he hadn't lied about his father's name; he would have liked to invoke it now and then. Jonah had also once warned young Vlad about the dangers of holding still. "Keep striding," he'd told him. "Always." Unfortunately, in stopping to impart to his son this particular particle of wisdom, he had himself been picked off the black water by a low-flying crow. Vlad remembered the feelings of first shock, then denial, then bereavement. But at least he'd been spared the sight of the shrinking corpse. Vlad shuddered. Both memories—old and new—jerked him back into the present. Wylie would bring up that shrinking question again. He was sure of it.

"Put a wiggle in it, Wy," he called out. His voice was stern now, protective, like a father. But his anger was gone. It was just that—how could he ever forgive himself if anything were to happen to that little bugger? He watched him skate in slow circles. "You still mad at me, Wy?"

Wylie didn't answer, just kept skating around. Uh oh. He was thinking again. Probably about something else that Vlad couldn't possibly answer. Like, why do we have six legs? Or, why do bees make that sound? Or, why do spiders shoot string from their butts? Or, why are ants always in such a rush? Or, why do humans get all fluttery around ladybugs, but throw rocks in the water at us?

"Vlad?" Wylie began.

Here it comes.

"Why do we digest our own wings?"

Vlad laughed. That was a new one. "Who told you that?"

"No one told me. I just know." Wylie found a worm that had wriggled into the water by mistake. He prepared to insert his rostrum into the flailing form. "And that's why," he said, "we can't fly."

Vlad skated over to join him for a snack. Worms were not his favorite—the texture too flabby, the juices too earthy for his taste—but they were still a lot better than the muddy mosquito larvae he'd been choking down for the last couple of days. "So if you know so much already," Vlad said, putting a fatherly tone into his voice, "what are you asking me for?"

Wylie pushed himself away.

Full already? What a waste, thought Vlad. He'd have to finish it himself.

"Just thought you might know," Wylie said.

Vlad kept on slurping up his meal, though he wasn't enjoying it much. What he'd give for a good butterfly, or even a damselfly, just then. Light and airy. Crunchy in all the right places. And pretty besides. As they say, presentation is everything.

"Vlad?" Wylie began again. "Why *do* we shrink up when we die?"

Vlad took one last wormy slurp. He'd been thinking about this question, so was not entirely unprepared. "Well," he said. "I'm guessing it has something to do with the parts of us we can't see."

"Which parts?"

"The invisible parts that live on the inside. I think they must go somewhere else when we die. So then our bodies get smaller." He paused to consider where that somewhere might be. Maybe up in the sky? Or maybe even on the other side of this watery membrane, where no strider had ever gone before. And lived to tell about it, that is. Hell, he didn't know. But he'd better think of something or Wylie would never let it rest.

Suddenly, the water surged around him. Vlad felt her before he saw her. Nadia. There in the rushes. Electric. His own invisible parts jumped up and down inside him.

Wylie had been listening intently. "Yes, inside. Invisible." He began skating in slow circles again. "It may be," he said, "very like the world that lies beneath the surface of the pond." He was thinking so hard that he nearly stopped skating. "Just because we can't see it, can't penetrate it, doesn't mean it doesn't exist."

"Yeah. Penetrate." Vlad was distracted. He was feeling, with his whole self, the erotic ripples of Nadia's nearness.

"And what if," said Wylie, "we could do more than just skim the surface? What if we could dive down, deeper, into the depths of the unknown?"

"We'd die," said Vlad, absently. Nadia's father and brother were nowhere in sight. "We're striders. That's what we do. Our feet were made for skating on surfaces. That's all."

"But what if we tried to dive? Just tried? How can we know for sure unless we try?"

Vlad was thinking the same thing. Nadia so near, and no other male in sight. What could be the harm of trying? "Dangerous," he whispered. But he moved in closer.

"Knowledge is fatal," Nadia said in a silky, slippery voice. But she didn't skate away.

"Fatal." Vlad didn't care. He felt as if a current were pulling him toward her. He couldn't stop.

"Vlad!" Wylie shouted. "Vlad, look!"

He looked up to see a damselfly in distress. It was falling, fluttering, trying in vain to escape the deadly water. Too late. One gossamer wing, then the other, touched the water's surface. For a moment, Vlad was torn between his appetites. But Nadia won out. Vladimir stayed put. "You get it," he called to Wylie. "Save me some."

"But Vlad!" Wylie shouted again. "You didn't look. Look at my feet! I'm doing it! I am!"

"Doing what," Vlad said, without looking. It was not the time for show and tell.

"Sinking," said Wylie, quietly.

"What?" Vlad looked up in time to see Wylie going under. He extricated himself from Nadia quickly, nearly losing some body parts in the process. "Hold on!" he shouted. "Kick! Move!"

"I see it," said Wylie. His voice was soft, amazed.

"Keep moving!" said Vlad. He sped to him, caught him by a back leg, fought against the wounded water, tried to close up the hole Wylie'd opened.

"Vlad! Look out!" It was Nadia who shouted that time. Vlad looked up to see a big ugly crow dive bombing right for them.

Vlad slipped, with Wylie, into the hole in the water. He opened his eyes. Watched the crow in slow motion through a watery lens. Up and away. Crows gave up so easily. "You okay?" he tried to ask Wylie, but his words were lost in a watery garble.

"I see it," said Wylie again. But his words were lost too.

"Kick! Kick!" urged Vlad.

Wylie shook his head. He was sinking. The filaments on his feet had absorbed too much water. They were pulling him down.

As were Vladimir's. He looked up to see Nadia's delicate tarsi rowing frantically overhead.

"Don't worry," said Wylie, as he gently wafted to the bottom of the pond. "I've been here before." He sounded content. "I'll be back." And then Vlad heard a watery version of his own father's voice say, "Keep striding, Vlad. Don't stop."

"Wy!" Vlad shouted, but he knew it was useless. So he poured the last of his energies into his own tarsi, and kicked for all he was worth.

He woke up on a lily pad. Nadia and Seth and Mr. Slide were skating around him, dipping and gliding back and forth, back and forth.

"He's waking up," said Mr. Slide.

"What was it like?" asked Seth.

Vlad didn't know. He'd been so busy trying to save Wylie and himself that he hadn't really paid attention. His one chance on the other side and he'd forgotten to look.

He just remembered some darkness. Then some light. Some glimmering, like a promise.

"Doesn't matter," said Nadia. "You've come back to us. It's a miracle."

It was. No other word for it. No strider had ever penetrated the surface before and survived.

Vlad missed Wylie. He'd never forget him. But Nadia stayed by his side now. Her father and brother appeared to be somewhat relieved, truth be told, to transfer to Vlad the responsibility of protecting the loveliest strider on the pond. So life was generally good for Vlad, what with Nadia, and the occasional damselfly treat, and of course, there was striding, striding, always striding, to do. But something had changed.

"You're shrinking," said Nadia one day. "You're smaller than you were. Why is that?"

It's because some part of my invisible inside skated away from me the minute I broke through the pond, went somewhere else, he wanted to tell her. But he couldn't tell her that.

"You're wrong," he told her. He'd become quite good at lying. "If I were shrinking, could I do this?" And then he took hold of her abdomen and gave her thrills and spills and pretty nymphs and everything she wanted so she might never have to live like Mrs. Bitterman.

Still, he had his own questions. And no one, now, to answer them. Wy? Where are you now? And what did you do with my inside self? And have we all lived before and will we all live again? And do striders really digest their own wings? Wy?

Victoria's Secret

Victoria was a single mom. But, through a clear-sighted assessment of her immediate situation, a carefully cultivated positivism, an iron-willed determination to achieve her goals at any cost, and an inherited tendency toward objectivity, she managed to avoid much of the bitterness and self-recrimination that all too often accompany that classification.

Looking back, Victoria had done everything that had been expected of a young female in her demographic. She'd been a model daughter; quiet, obedient, and attentive to her duties. She'd listened respectfully to everything the queen-mother had told her, had simply nodded her heart-shaped head even when the queen's most frequent adage—"One does what one must"—assaulted her early idealism. And when the time came, in spite of her personal feelings, Victoria had obligingly grown her wings and swarmed up with her brothers and sisters to mate. Then she'd submitted to the most attractive male, as was her right and privilege as a full-blooded Leaf-cutting Ant, and she certainly had never blamed her mate for doing what he did then—i.e. die—right after they'd consummated their union. Then she'd flown back down to earth, as was expected, shed her wings, and set to work. And it was this realization—that she had done every single task required of her with dignity and a willing heart—that had gotten her through the most daunting days of her new life as a single mother and the trials that were to follow.

It was frightening in the beginning, even though she'd followed the queen-mother's directives to the letter. As instructed, Victoria had carried a bit of the family fungus in her mouth to the nuptials, nourished it with her own fecal matter, and had laid her first brood in its warmly growing midst. But the laying of eggs was something she felt that one could never be fully prepared for. It took so long, was one thing. And that there were so very many of them—over one hundred eggs first time out—was another. The pain was something else, but she had been trained to bear pain, hardship, heartache. One did what one must, for the good of the colony.

After they hatched, she sent ten of her firstborn out to gather leaf fragments. "Now march!" she told them. "And don't you dare come back without them." As queen, it was important to be authoritative—the future of their new fungus garden and, by extension, their very existence, depended upon it.

"Good job," she said, stoutly, as they returned. It was important to avoid over-praising the workers, but they did look so cute marching back in single file, carrying their leaf fragments overhead like little parasols. She was proud of her first brood—what was left of them—though she quickly checked herself, recalling the dangers of maternal tenderness. She was queen, first and foremost. They were workers. One does what one must. They would all do their part to make the colony a success.

So Victoria got to laying again. One hundred more eggs. This time, she sent out twenty new workers, along with the original ten. One hundred more eggs. The workers had all grown larger, stronger, from the increased richness of their fungus garden. One hundred more. And she was growing larger too. Plumper, more regal, though she never touched fungus herself—didn't like what it did to her mood swings. One hundred more. This time, when the workers returned, she sent two hundred of them to dig chambers and tunnels. They'd need those chambers very soon, for storage, for aeration, to hide from the inevitable predators. "Destroy anything that gets in your way," she instructed. "Be on the lookout, in particular, for those flabby little earth-wrigglers. They may look all soft and squishy, but they'll worm their way right into our territory—mark my words—and they'll undermine everything we've built." She made herself larger for the last admonition. "And dig those tunnels deep," she said, sternly. "Or you'll be sorry."

It was strange, to some of the workers, that Victoria felt the need to always add that extra threat at the end of her instructions. It wasn't as if they had ever disobeyed, or ever stopped working. One rusty little ant named Rufus said, "I wonder what would happen if we didn't strip the trees or dig the tunnels?" But to most of the thousands of workers it was purely a rhetorical question; they shrugged, went back to their tasks. Their colony mound had grown to over a kublick by this point, and their tunnels extended ten full kublicks below ground.

"Not for us to ask questions," said Horace, a large, brown ant who'd always lacked imagination.

"Maybe she'd *eat* us," joked Cody, a strapping young ant of the most recent brood. He was prone to be clownish.

Rufus laughed with him then, but a few of the old-timers—those who were starting to grow weary of their endless burdens—didn't let the question die. "I'm not absolutely certain," said Elizabeth, a first-brood female who was getting a little tired, and perhaps not a little jealous, of the queen-mother, "but didn't we have a lot more brothers and sisters when we started out?" And her siblings agreed that they had. "One of us ought to go ask her what happened to *them*," said Elizabeth, and they all agreed. But nobody volunteered.

By the time the mound had grown two kublicks tall, the tunnels had expanded into more than twenty kublicks of underground chambers, and the worker force had multiplied to nearly ten thousand extremely diligent individuals, the original brood was feeling increasingly unappreciated. "We're just numbers to her now," Elizabeth said. "Somebody ought to ask her what happened to our original brothers and sisters!" Still, nobody volunteered. "Nothing to lose at this point," she said, more loudly. Elizabeth was beginning to feel a bit cheated that she'd never been chosen to grow wings, or to mate in a swarm, or to start her own colony. "That old witch gets fatter every day." She spat out her elderberry leaf as if it were hemlock.

"You go ahead," said Horace. "Ask her." He picked up the leaf she'd spat out and went to work on it with his own mandibles. "Tell us what you find out."

"Cowards!" she said, though they all just kept chewing. She tossed her antennae and turned sharply on her back tarsomeres. "I hope you choke."

It took Elizabeth longer than she expected to find the queen-mother. Her echo-locator had never been as sharp as her mandibles, so it had always fallen to Elizabeth to do the stripping and chewing, rather than the burrowing and navigating. By the time she had negotiated the glebs and glebs of winding tunnels and chambers, in fact, she was feeling a bit claustrophobic and somewhat grateful, truth be told, to be a worker instead of a queen. She stopped from time to time to munch on fungus, but just enough to keep her strength up—she was somewhat vain of her tiny waist.

At last, the grandest chamber. Elizabeth felt a bit covetous again, but was placated when she saw the enormous bulk of the queen-mother. (I may be unappreciated and unfulfilled, she said to herself, but at least I'm not fat.) Victoria's enormous back was turned, so Elizabeth took advantage of the moment to gaze deeply at the splendor of a queen's chamber. The handsomest young soldier ants—the queen's own secret service—were scurrying to and fro, cooling her, warming her, servicing her, probably, though Elizabeth couldn't imagine that process, given her mother's astonishing bulk and their diminutive size.

Elizabeth tiptoed in closer. She saw enormous piles of white eggs in one corner of the chamber, piles of larvae in another. The queen-mother was munching on something—as if that old cow needed any more food—but Elizabeth couldn't quite see what it was and she didn't want to get too close.

"Who's there?" bellowed the queen-mother. The handsome soldiers froze in their tracks. Elizabeth froze too.

"Just me," she said. "Elizabeth. Remember me?" She tiptoed a little closer, but the fiercely protective soldiers sprang to life, surrounding her. "I came all this way just to ask you a question. May I speak?"

Victoria motioned for her guards to disperse. "Well, you're a scrawny little thing, aren't you." White matter was falling from her mouth.

Elizabeth held her tongue. To be insulted by such a huge . . . well, no matter. "Yes, I am," she said, somewhat proudly.

The queen took a closer look. It pleased her to hear the pride in her daughter's voice. "Bravo," said the queen. She finished chewing and swallowed hard. A long-buried maternal tenderness resurfaced, but she fought it down bravely. "Well?" she said. "What is your question?"

Elizabeth moved closer. "It's just that, some of us were wondering . . . that is, some of us remembered . . ." she crept closer as she spoke—she strained to see what kinds of delicacies a queen was privileged to eat—". . . brothers and sisters from long ago, and we wondered, well, what happened to them?"

Victoria had indulged her daughter's approach, had softened, in fact, at this evidence of her daughter's courage. But at the presumption of the question itself, she re-hardened into her full, queenly imperiousness. "One does what one must."

Elizabeth began to ask another way, thinking herself misunderstood, but then she stopped, looked around again. "Oh," she said, fitting it all together at last—the eggs, the larva, the enormity of her mother. She started to back away.

Victoria took a new mouthful of white eggs, chewed them slowly, deliberately. She let the juice run freely from her mandibles as Elizabeth watched. Then she signaled to her soldiers with a twitch of her antennae.

They closed in, carried the terrified Elizabeth to their queen. "You should not have abandoned your duties, Elizabeth. You should not have come here. Or seen this." The soldiers locked Elizabeth in their collective grip as she struggled and clawed at the desperate air. They marched her straight to Victoria's powerful jaws. "For the good of the colony," said the queen.

"Please, please, my mother, please," cried Elizabeth as she watched the jaws unhinge.

Victoria paused. "My dear child," she whispered. Then she clamped down cleanly, mercifully. She tore and chewed and swallowed—hard. Her wide eyes glistened with regal tears.

Meanwhile, in Ithaca . . .

Sing in me, O Muse! That I might tell the tale of he who braved Poseidon's wrath and fought the Fates themselves (when he wasn't entangled in the lovely arms of a nymph, or hurling his hubris at one-eyed monsters, or dipping his toes in the River Styx) to return to the wife and son from whom he had been so tragically wrenched. Help me, O Muse, in language exalted, dignified, and epithet-laced, to make his story true, and large, as befitting an epic hero of his lofty stature.

But Muse, first, eavesdrop with me, will you, on the female that he left behind? How she lights up her web! There is another tale here I think—romantic, inspiring—but what can it be? So often the female's voice is muted and hushed or hidden behind the words of a male.

But I'm not telling you anything you don't already know, Muse, am I.

And I'm not, Zeus knows, trying to interject my own agenda, but might I suggest that we begin our story in media res, with the wily Odysseus already weeping for his lost life on the shores of Phoenicia, with the young Telemakus off nursing his identity crisis in the palace of the good King Menelaus and his whore-wife Helen, with the grey-eyed Athena still scheming and pleading with the uber-Gubs to let our hero return, and with the gracious Penelope still waiting?

Just waiting. Patient as a rock. Virtuous as an angel. There she is. A golden beauty, long-legged and luminous. An orb-spinner of the most refined lineage. I am half in love with her myself. Not that she is nearly as wondrous as you are, dear Muse. Not even almost.

Get to the point, you say? Of course. I am your servant.

Standing before our lovely queen is Antinous, the most despicable of all the suitors. A real cad. But handsome. Yes. Perhaps the most dashingly handsome one of the lot.

"Marry me, fair lady of the web!"

   "Marry? You?"

   "Yes! Now! And I will bring you ..."

It's difficult to hear his words, isn't it, Muse? He keeps his pedipalp so unnervingly close to his chelicerae. He really should state his propositions more clearly.

And the gentle Penelope speaks to him sharply—which is appropriate, under the circumstances, don't you think?

"I am already married, Antinous. Have you forgotten?"

   "To a wanderer. A philanderer. And he has been gone so long."

   "Tell me about it."

   "You deserve better, my lady."

He is a sly one, that Antinous. A flatterer. But he has a point. Yes, sorry, Muse. I will be quiet. No need to call Zeus. I'll just sit here and listen. And watch. Take notes. No more interrupting.

"I mean only that I sympathize with your position, my queen. A magnificent specimen like yourself, all alone, day after day, night after night. Tell me, my lady, how do you fill your hours?"

   "I wait. I weave."

   Antinous lifts his sticky palps and gingerly circles the queen. "Rumor has it that you unweave as well." He notices her expression then and backs away judiciously. "Every night. When no one's looking."

"Weaving," she says. "Unweaving. It's all the same thing."

"But one is creating and one is destroying." Antinous swells up a bit at the profundity of his own observation. "How can you say they're the same thing?"

"Call it whatever you want to." Penelope draws in two of her golden legs. "Words matter little."

"But I didn't make up the words," he says, pouncing on his advantage.

"Nor did I, Antinous. Nor did I make up this world, nor our places within it."

Antinous stops fidgeting, becomes completely still. It is best to be still sometimes, particularly when your companion is twice your size and is beginning to show signs of agitation.

You're absolutely correct, my Muse. I was editorializing. It's a bad habit that I'm trying to break. Distracting, yes. And yes, I suppose I do have some biases against Antinous that become apparent through my word choice. But how can he take advantage of such a lovely and long-suffering creature? Can't he see that her longing for Odysseus has colored her responses? Hasn't she been through enough already? But you are right, as always, my Muse. Objectivity is extremely important. Thank you for correcting me. I'll try harder.

"And creation and destruction are really quite different," she adds.

"That's what I just said."

"But in actuality," says Penelope, "they're exactly the same."

"My queen," says Antinous. "How can that be? You just finished saying that . . ."

"Do I contradict myself? Very well then, I contradict myself. I am large. I contain multitudes."

"Well, you ARE large," says Antinous.

"And you are a stupid little spider," says the queen. "Small in every way." She draws in two more long, golden legs. "If only Odysseus were here," she says, sadly.

"Multitudes? What do you mean, you contain multitudes?"

"Of suitors, Antinous. Suitors. Go away please. You have already ransacked my stores and abused my hospitality. Just you wait until Odysseus gets home."

"You contain them?"

Penelope sighs. "Of course, Antinous. I am like my husband that way. Kind to my followers, but ruthless to my enemies. That's just how we spin."

"But what . . ."

"Surely even you must have heard of that universal truth, Antinious. That we have contempt for whatever there are too many of."

"Even suitors?"

"Especially suitors. And each one of them was way too needy."

"But my queen, if I may be so bold, perhaps each was seeking just some simple companionship." Antinous has been trying to lift his palps, but the more he struggles, the more he sticks.

Penelope points to her web. "Sorry about that," she says. "That interminable waiting for Odysseus to return, for my life to begin, changed me inside. I mean, in ways that weren't quite natural. Take my silk, for instance. It's much stickier than it ought to be." She shrugs. "Simple physiology," she says. "But to return to your point about 'companionship.' There is nothing simple about companionship, Antinous, as you know very well. Look at how many of your companions you have already betrayed. And if Odysseus hopped up on this web right now, you'd betray me in a heartbeat—you know you would—just to save your own miserable little exoskeleton."

Antinous touches his chelicerae coyly with one newly extricated pedipalp. "You can't blame a guy for putting himself first."

Penelope unfurls her legs as she speaks and regains some of her radiance. "Can't I? Would a female do that? And anyway, it wasn't companionship that your cohorts wanted. They wanted simply to get into my epigynum, and to help themselves to my treasures. That's all. Same as you."

"My queen, I'd never."

Penelope draws herself up to her full queenly height. "Yes, do deny it, Antinous. Deny it to the very end. Why start honoring the truth at this point? You're so much sexier when you lie."

What's she doing now, O Muse? How shall I describe the way she circles and circles the hapless Antinous? I almost feel sorry for him. She's tying him up; toying with him! Seducing him, is what she's doing. Are you watching this, Muse? Using the promise of sex to lure him into her trap. Most unseemly for a female, don't you think? I'm afraid we may lose the sympathy of our readers. Well, yes, I suppose you are right about that. Cruelty shouldn't be more disturbing in a female than it is in a male. There is a double standard there. Indeed. And yet, I can't help feeling that it's wronger, somehow. Is that a word? Wronger?

"You really should have left me, Antinous—as did my dear wandering husband—when I gave you the chance. But do not worry. I won't kill you right away. I'll allow you to linger a while longer. I think you're kind of cute. And I won't make you suffer—much. Time is on my side at last. I'll tell you all my secrets first. What do they matter now? You've always liked secrets. You've kept a good many from me, I know. But you'll have your chance to disgorge yours too, if you like. I can be a very good listener. I've had a great deal of practice. But you'll want to relax your spermaphore, my lord. It's going nowhere now, I assure you. Now that I have you're attention, I'll tell you my secrets. No, no. Don't speak. You'll have your turn. Just listen:

"I loved my husband, yes. I loved him on an epic scale—I would have gladly given him my life. But he refused that gift. He wanted more. He wanted me to postpone my life until it suited him to let me live again. He required me to deny each one of my todays, each one of my tomorrows, in breathless anticipation of that shining, mythical, future moment when he finally decided to complete me with his presence. Now, now. Stop wriggling. Anger? I suppose I have some anger, yes. But what has that to do with you? With us? Be patient now. I have so much more to tell you.

"I love him still, is the problem. Or rather, I love the Odysseus who feigned madness to remain by my side. It wasn't his fault, wily though he was, that his trick was discovered. I remind myself of that sometimes. Telemakus reminds me too. There can be no easy answers. But I can't know if I'll love the Odysseus who comes home to me again. If he comes home to me again. I'm not the same Penelope he left behind.

"In fact, I am so much more and so much less than Odysseus's wife now. I have been waiting for him so long that the waiting itself has been woven into my very glands, as you saw for yourself. And my spinnerets. They are lovely spinnerets, aren't they? I've seen you eyeing them. Don't think I haven't. But hush, Antinous. If you interrupt again I may have to impale you sooner rather than later and be done with it. Listen: I am pure aloneness now. I have guarded my aloneness—as indeed my own Odysseus may have once wanted to guard my corporeal self—with cunning and ferocity. Relentlessly. Unwaveringly. I polished and sharpened my aloneness into my grandest possession and my most reliable weapon. I don't lean, you may have noticed. Not on anyone. For a while there, I longed to. But not any more."

O sing to me, O Muse, that I might hear your voice instead of Penelope's. I fear the queen has come unhinged.

"Odysseus would be foolish to think that his presence, after all this time, could ever refill the hole his absence made in my heart. I am hungry, hungrier than you could ever imagine. There now, Antinous. Time to turn you upside down. You don't mind dangling there for a moment, do you? I have just a few more details to make ready.

"And he'd be foolish, too, to imagine that I would have remained forever helpless and clingy—though I once was that, too—or that I would have left it to him alone to avenge the injustices, the abuses I have suffered."

"My lady, I . . ."

"Yes, yes, Antinous. Am I making it too tight? Here, I'll loosen it a little. Better? Did you think that I was tricked by your silky words and your soft black eyes into believing that you ever cared for me? Or for my son either?

"I do. I did . . ."

"I saved you for the last. I confess, I did enjoy your company. You are clever in your hypocrisy and more fun to watch than most. And you are a very pretty spider, for all your poison."

"But I assure you, my queen . . ."

"And I did believe you sometimes. I did. Sometimes I did."

"Because I meant what . . ."

"Of course that only made your betrayals that much less palatable."

Stop her, Muse! I can't watch. Can't we go find Calypso instead? There's a pretty nymph—she turns Odysseus free. Can't we just jump forward a bit, until Odysseus returns? That way, we can watch justice being served in a manly and straightforward manner, the way it's supposed to happen. What's that? Death is the Mother of Beauty, you say? What's that supposed to mean? It doesn't even make any sense. Say, you're on her side, aren't you? Figures. The Furies. The Fates. All those sororities. Dames always stick together. Sorry. Sorry. I didn't mean that. You know I didn't. No need to tell Zeus. He has enough to deal with already. Hera, for instance. Athena, Aphrodite, that crazy, ball-busting, forest-ranger chick, Diana. Sorry. Sorry. Didn't mean that either. Of course Diana has every right to choose her own lifestyle. But Muse, look at Penelope! What's that she's doing to him now? I can't watch. But I can't look away.

"Struggle all you like, Antinous. But wait. You haven't told me your secrets yet. I promised you I'd listen and I will. What's that? You don't feel like talking? How strange. How unlike you. But suit yourself. It's your funeral. Let's see. I want to do this right. Let me pull you just a little bit more to my . . . there. Right there. That's how Odysseus would have done it and I'll certainly respect my heroic husband's wishes. But he won't mind, I don't think, if I add my own twist. Yes? Does it hurt? Poor thing. Here, let me make it tighter. You yellow cur, you die in blood. Not dead yet? Oh dear. A pity. Let's try again. Take heart, Antinous. You always were my favorite."

Right. Death is the Mother of Beauty. I heard you the first time. Deep, Muse. Real deep. You probably didn't even make it up yourself. Hey, I got one for you. Bros before hoes.

Sweet Jesus, where'd that ladybug come from? Hasn't that sadistic queen had enough for one day? Fly away home, little one! Probably fell off that rose bush, poor kid. Yeah, I got me a conscience, Muse. Like it or not.

"Jesus?" Not sure where that came from, but I've got a weird feeling it's going to be important one day. Yeah, I guess I've got a few secrets of my own, Muse. I know a few things, even without you breathing your divine, garlic-scented inspiration in my face.

You can tell Zeus I quit. I'm done. What gives, Odysseus? This was supposed to be your story. You'd better get home, bro. And quick. You'll never believe what your wife has been up to.

Ladybug Lullabies

Ladybug, come you here and stand
Upon my hand; I will not harm you
And nothing need alarm you.
Why don't you spread your little wings?
Tiny dainty colored things—
Black and orange, red and yellow,
Pretty fellow!

Leslie considered his next move. He'd already dropped that annoying little Victor on a web and left him to his fate. Ordinarily, he would have dispatched the child himself, but Victor's elytra (as he knew all too well from experience with Victor's siblings) was entirely too bland for his taste. Virtually inedible, that whole bourgeois family. And that kid just wouldn't shut up. He would've blown Leslie's whole operation.

If it wasn't blown already. Leslie reminded himself that paranoia was not becoming in a middle-aged—although still undeniably charming—ladybug. Still, he felt the suspicions of his community swarm around him, thick as mayflies. And it might not be long before the accusations started flying as well. He was starting to get edgy. Some of his neighboring coleoptera were showing signs of actually missing their children. Difficult to imagine, but the evidence was indisputable. Their spots were fading, for one thing. And just the other day, Leslie with his own cuticular lenses observed a few of them plod right over a succulent cluster of aphids without even pausing for a snack. And at least one of them—James, dear and loyal James, with his tedious morality, et tu James?—might even be on to him. Nearly inconceivable, but not quite. Alas. Leslie conceded that he may have occasionally underestimated their individual intelligences. They certainly had underestimated his.

He paused to indulge in some particularly sticky aphid snacks. Tasty, yes. But strangely unsatisfying. Perhaps he was mourning, too? Leslie thought of the children. He got warm all over, in fact, when he remembered the little ones at their games. Hide and Seek. Lost and Found. And the songs he used to sing them. Fly away home! Tiny, dainty things, indeed. Darlings, they were. So fresh. So small. Delicious.

Leslie sighed. The times, they were achanging. He was about to retreat for the afternoon, to consider, perhaps, in the quiet of his own burrow, the possibility of amending his ways before it was too late. But then he overheard two of them talking. About *him,* no less. It was more than rude. And it was that pathetic Reeta creature, as well. The one he'd deigned to honor with his attentions, just the other day.

"The way he looks at me," Reeta told her friend. "The way he . . ." she shuddered, mid-idea.

For mercy's sake, Leslie thought, finish your sentence, you saggy-gutted, soppy-minded female. Ever heard of a fragment? How DO I look at you? He wanted to shout it, but controlled himself, as always.

Her squatty friend sidled up to Reeta. "He's morally, as well as sexually . . ."—here she paused to search the ground, apparently for exactly the right word—"dubious." She lit up then, understandably proud.

Well, well, thought Leslie. Most impressive. He decided to reveal himself. He turned on the charm then—made himself the brightest ladybug red in the garden. It had always worked in the past—dazzled the thoughts right out of their feeble little brains. And sure enough, the minute Reeta saw him, she trotted right over and stood at his side. But what was this? Resistance from the squatty one? Did she have a mind after all?

He dared hope, for a moment, that she might. Resist me, he urged her. Save yourself. Perhaps there would be hope then. For him, and for all of them. Perhaps this was the one female who would be able to do for him what all the others—his mother included—had not. Perhaps this was the female who could help him actualize a wholesome identity—a real, true, viable identity— in this sexually ambiguous world of male *lady*bugs and female *man*tids. It had bothered him all of his life. What kind of a god had conceived of a planet where creatures were doomed to carry crosses they did not, themselves, construct? He considered all this as he watched the squatty one decide. Galatea, he named her in his own imagination. Oh, gallant one. His own creation. Her physical stumpiness transformed itself into a wondrous solidity of resolve. Outstanding female! Resist me to the end! And in your resistance, lend me your own moral lantern to light my way back to a world of goodness and peace.

But she faltered. Her antennae picked up something in the air and twitched, trembled. She caved. At least she made her way with dignity, Leslie told himself. That was something. At least she didn't scurry. But she made her way to his side, nonetheless. Stood there, with Reeta. Stupidly awaiting her fate. Her antennae kept trembling.

Females, Leslie fumed. Always the same. Worse than children. He cast his net and they fell in. Even Galatea. She was a figment of his imagination only. She was just another ladybug—no conflicts for her!—just like all the others. His disappointment was so great that he nearly lost his appetites. But not quite. "You betrayed me," he said to the stubby one. But she showed no signs of understanding—just moved closer to his brilliant red elytra. This enraged him, but he kept his emotions in check. Not yet, he told himself. Wait. Females. Worthless progenitors of a worthless species. They deserved what they got. He led them down to his burrow. Gave it to them both.

Afterwards, when he crawled back up into the light again, somewhat sick at heart and a little nauseous, he found James waiting for him on a purple azalea.

"Where have you been," James demanded.

Leslie chuckled. "You sound like a jealous wife."

James flushed a dark crimson. "I need to know where you've been."

"There, there." Leslie approached him, stroked him with his antennae. "There's a good boy."

James quieted immediately, his elytra restored to its natural pinkish color. How easy that was, thought Leslie. This is why he'd always preferred males. No romantic nonsense attached. No impossible hopes that their intellects might even be capable of soaring up there with his own. Simple males. Stupid males. Easy, easy. "Easy there, Sweet Baby James."

But James pulled away. "Do you have to be so condescending all that time? Even when I'm trying to . . ." His color began to rise again. "You know what you are? You're nothing but a self-loathing ladybug."

Leslie backed up. "Why, James. Those are big words for you. Will you say them again? Pretty please?"

"You heard me."

"I can't believe . . ."

"Well, believe," said James. "Because I mean it." He turned around, stretched his silvery wings, then pulled them back in again. His next words were nearly inaudible. "I know what you've done." He turned in circles, around and around. "I know about all of it."

Leslie took a moment to recover. A brief flit of fear, then the fury surged. Wait, Leslie told himself. There. Here comes the pity. Poor James. Poor, good, simple boy. He was just telling the truth. He had some idea that truth had been called for. That truth could somehow right things. Leslie extended a gentle antenna, but James again pulled away. "I'm sorry," Leslie said, and he really was. For what he had done, and for what he would do again, as soon as the opportunity presented itself. But he would not be deterred. Certainly not by this innocent young ingrate whom he'd not only spared but had taken in, nurtured, cared for. Loved.

James surprised him with his strength. Fighting back? Good for you, boy! Fight away! But it was no use. Leslie was practiced at cruelty, while James hadn't, finally, the stomach for it. "Everyone knows about you," James whispered, at the end. But just before Leslie finished him, a webby something pinned them both down and then scooped, swooped them up high into the air. Their neighbors were captured as well—in flight, on porch swings, on camellia blossoms, on ragged tree trunks, and soon Leslie, James, little Lucie, and the twins and all their siblings, aunts and uncles, and parents, found themselves tossed together into a slippery container, jumbled, tumbled, bumping, sliding against one another's slick coats, terrified and dizzied by the assault. Anselmo lost his wings in the chaos, Millie, her legs. But by and large they were mostly intact. And they had enough air, enough food. At least for a while.

They settled down then, letting themselves be jostled and jiggled on some noisy conveyance that was not, once they accepted it, entirely unpleasant. One by one, they regained their voices. And one by one, they offered theories regarding the source of these, their latest troubles. Conspiracies. Divine retribution. Fate. Scapegoats. "Pipe down," growled old Mr. Bataglioni, with his customary authority. "He's right," said Doodle. "No fighting. We gotta stick together." The other beetles all murmured agreement. Everyone loved Doodle.

Except for Nick. Nick's elytra bore the scars of one too many scuffles with uncooperative thorn bushes; he didn't let anyone tell him what to do. He waited for the crowd to get quiet, and then he said, "I ain't stickin' together with no perv." His words floated inside the container but every beetle heard them and added their own mumbled echoes: "Pervert." "Murderer." "Pedophile." "Cannibal." Leslie feigned sleep, but listened intently. What if they'd figured it out? And there he was, exposed, with no exit strategy whatsoever.

The rumbling movement stopped. Scraps of angry phrases littered the silence as they were once again lifted and shaken, and then finally settled on something high and solid. The brightness flicked off—they were left in the dark.

"Put a lid on it," said old Mr. Bataglioni, but his voice sounded a good deal weaker in the darkness.

"I'm with Nick on this one," whispered Sadie, who had recently lost six children in as many days. She set aside her housewifely voice and allowed an edge of hysteria to creep in. "And that pervert is curled up right over there, innocent as you please. When everyone knows he . . . he . . ."

Mrs. Lacombe rushed to her side. "Judge not, lest ye be judged." But Mrs. Lacombe had lost children of her own when they were no more than grubs, and it was hard sometimes, to be charitable.

"Bleeding heart liberals," growled Anselmo. "What about justice? What about the bad guys getting theirs?" Anselmo charged at Leslie, but he'd forgotten about his missing wings and was disappointed at how little stir he created. He was even more chagrined when Sadie herself—the very female he was trying to champion— stepped in to help him.

"Stop it!" shouted Doodle. "Violence is never the answer!"

"Doodle's right," Anselmo said, primarily to Sadie. "Everyone's tired. We ain't even thinkin' straight." And everyone, because they were tired, and because they were embarrassed for Anselmo, agreed.

"There'll be time to talk in the morning," said Doodle.

They all went to sleep then, uneasily at first, but then heavily, deeply. All except James. His elytra had been cracked in his fight with Leslie, and he felt his life juices slowly slipping away. But he stood guard over Leslie nonetheless, all night long, just in case Nick or Anselmo or Sadie or anyone else got any ideas.

Morning broke with a sharp flick of hard light and a harsh human call. The ladybugs remained silent, too cold and cramped and frightened to do anything but lie still in their packaged stupor. Little Lucie whispered "where are we?" and Mrs. Lacombe fought down the urge to say "in Hell." Occasionally, one ladybug would inadvertently bump into another, trying to find a way to stretch his wings, before he remembered where he was. Anselmo itched to get the fight going again. Mr. Bataglioni told him to shut up his fool mouth.

The harsh human voices turned to gentler ones, and the sharp light softened. But it was getting hard to breathe in the container and the food was running out. Sadie caressed little Lucie with her antennae, even though she wasn't her own cuticle and blood. "Stay close, child," she said. "I'll protect you."

Just then, their container was lifted again, but gently. "I'm taking you home with me," a female human crooned, and after being manhandled once more, passed over flashing lights with a piercing beep, then jostled in yet another moving conveyance, their container was placed on something that felt soft and lumpy and familiar. "I smell green," said little Lucie.

"So many aphids on my beautiful morning glories!" The human lifted the container up to her eyes, gazed on its occupants. "I'm counting on you guys," she said as she opened the lid. Doodle was the first to fly away. "Hey! Wait a minute," the human said. But one by one, the ladybugs unfurled in the sunshine and took to the sky. Most of them flew away fast, like Doodle, but some, like Sadie and little Lucie and Mrs. Lacombe stayed put on the morning glories out of gratitude to the human—or female solidarity—or hunger—and joyfully munched away on the troublesome aphids. A few, like old Mr. Bataglioni, stayed because they were old enough to know that "out there" was rarely as sweet as "right here" and because flying was not as easy as it used to be. Some of them stayed because, like Anselmo, they had no choice, and some of them, like Nick, stayed because they had scores to settle with bug-buggers and other perceived blights on the natural world. But one of them, James, stayed behind just to stand beside the one individual who would never have stood beside him.

"Where do you think *you're* going," Nick called to Leslie as he crawled up the side of the container. Anselmo flanked Nick and tried to block Leslie's way, but dared not charge again.

"Wherever the wind takes me," was Leslie's response. He could see, quite clearly, it was time to move on.

"Oh yeah?" said Nick. "And what about your little girlfriend, here?" They wedged James between them. "You gonna leave him to take the rap for you?"

James gazed up at Leslie. "Save yourself," James told him, with a brief, brave flicker of pink.

Leslie suspected that he probably should have been moved by the selflessness of James' declaration—that some noble act of heroism on his own part was probably called for. He cast a sideways glance at James, and he pitied him again—he really did. But the day was warm and his wings were strong and he'd always wanted to travel. "'Fraid I can't stay," said Leslie, "much as I'd love to." He paused on the edge of the container. For a moment, he imagined that he'd worked his charms again, and that Nick and Anselmo were just going to give up then and leave James alone. But that wasn't the case. Too bad. James was a very good ladybug. He certainly didn't deserve to die for Leslie's own sins. But what could Leslie do? James was dying anyway and it would be a shame to scar his own perfectly red elytra in some perfectly futile gesture. Even James would agree, he felt certain.

So Leslie flew up to one startlingly blue morning glory and took just one quick fortifying gulp of aphid before lifting off into the wild blue whatever, and he willed himself, wisely, to avoid looking back at poor James as those two hoodlums closed in to redeem their ever-challenged maleness. Most uncivilized behavior, he decided. Positively barbarian. And then Leslie congratulated himself, as he scanned the horizon, on having had the good sense to get out of that neighborhood before it went downhill entirely.

Old Dan's Lament: A Villanelle

My Love—not Sweet, but True,
Is all I had to make her stay.
I'd done all a dung beetle could do.

Just *merde* and mud—me through and through;
Still, my smell did not drive her away
From Love—not Sweet, but True.

Ah miracle, that she did not view
Her yellow wrong against my gray!
I'd done all a dung beetle could do.

My gifts, though, were so very few,
And all too soon she flew away
From Love—not Sweet, but True.

And with regret I must review
The Love I suffered to convey—
Did I all a dung beetle could do?

And yet I still would n'er undo
The magic that once bade her stay
With Love—not Sweet, but True.
I've done all a dung beetle can do.

The Rape of Persephone

Regret. That most powerful poison. Persephone shivered among the skeletonized carcasses that littered the floor of their kingdom. Her memories flew back to the warm, fennel-filled days of her youth—to the harmonious life she'd shared with other tumbling flower beetles like herself; to the happy chatter of her sisters as they tumbled together from flower to flower; to that one good soul who had pursued her, loved her, left her.

Dear Dan. How foolish she'd been. So full of misguided righteousness, so smug in her narrow beliefs. She'd fancied herself to be somehow better, nobler, than those promiscuous mayflies—and yet she'd sold her own self to the first good-looking, fast-talking, sexy male who eyed her. And cheaply too. Persephone nudged aside the shriveled caterpillar Hale had dragged down into their hellhole the night before. And to think she'd once thought herself too good for Dan. It seemed so funny now. But that's why she'd let him go. Well, that, and his smell. His smell had been hard to get used to. But he was such a good-hearted beetle. Dear Dan. Where are you? Take a look at your stuck-up little sweetheart now.

No, don't. Persephone would die if Dan ever saw her like this. She searched the carcass-strewn floor for one spot of unoccupied earth on which to lay her weary pronotum. Oh, how she would have welcomed the smell of good clean dung over this sickly-sweet odor—death. In the air, in the dirt, in her own filthy bristles. (The very bristles Dan had once praised for their bright softness.) And it was not natural death either. It was murder. Most foul.

How ironic it all seemed now. That Persephone would be drawn to Hale precisely because he was so very different from Dan! Because Dan, she saw now, had wounded her vanity and had hurt her heart too. And then Hale appeared—a dark answer to her prayer. There was nothing solid or reliable about Hale. Hale made her quiver. He was a whirlwind of raw lust and he'd swept her off her tarsi. He was glamorous in that bad-boy, dark and swarthy way, and the first time she saw him, she tumbled down, down, into an abyss of hopeless longing. And an abyss was just what it turned out to be. A great, gaping chasm of desperate attraction. And once she'd fallen, he'd kept her down—way down, beside him. She'd mistaken that for love.

And that whole rape/kidnapping story—just a myth she'd invented to keep from disappointing her parents. She knew there'd be words if they'd known the truth. So she cast herself as the victim in their eyes, when it had actually been her decision to seek him out, drawn as she was to the danger in his scent, to the intoxicating novelty of his very genus. An assassin bug. She'd never known anyone like him.

How long ago that seemed. Persephone missed her mother.

But her breeding ran deep and she'd been raised with the understanding that one finished what one started, and she had been the one who'd started this whole dark romance, and it wasn't *his* fault that she'd led him to believe she could be happy living like this. It had been different in the beginning. Back then, she hadn't understood that the sloughs of insects that decorated his chambers had once been living, fully metamorphosed individuals. She hadn't fully understood Hale's role in all that, or that his powerfully curved rostrum—the very one she'd once caressed appreciatively—was the instrument he used to suck the life-juice out of these unfortunate souls.

But once she got it, she got it. And then, everything changed.

Hale couldn't understand her repugnance. "I thought you liked my equipment," he said. "I thought that made you hot." And when she shook her pronotum no, and backed away, his aspect became menacing. He scared her, deeply. But it was her own fault, she told herself. She'd hurt his pride with her refusal, and any male might have reacted the same. So after that she strove to be a better partner—more acquiescent, less confrontational. But always, after that, if she did the smallest thing wrong—stacked the corpses inexpertly, or worse, got nervous and started tumbling around—he would thrust his rostrum in her face and say "I'd sure as hell hate to have to use this on *you*, baby." And then as a type of apology, follow it up with, "You know that, now, don't you?"

So Persephone became more and more nervous, needless to say. All day when he was gone, she would strive to control her tumbling habit. She trained herself to freeze, when she most wanted to tumble. And when she succeeded in sublimating her most primal instinct, she'd reward herself with small memory trips to springtime and family and Dan's amorous attentions. But when she failed, she made herself tumble over and over the stinking carcasses and she'd admonish herself sternly. "See! That's what you get for being stupid and undisciplined. That's just what you deserve." She was starting to dislike herself a great deal. She sometimes hoped that Hale would just go ahead and pierce her shapely cephalothorax with his beak and suck out her life-juice too. He'd already sucked out the best part of her.

In front of others, however, Persephone was every inch the queen of Hale's kingdom. There were things that happened between a male and a female that were simply not to be shared. And besides, she'd once confided her sorrows to an ambush bug named Stephen, having mistaken his bright yellow coat for evidence of kindness. Unfortunately, he'd misread her need for one of a different sort, and once she'd clarified the nature of their friendship, he turned around and spilled all her secrets to Hale. And he made up some secrets too, out of pure meanness and to align himself with Hale, she guessed, in brotherly solidarity against the treachery of females. This resulted, unfortunately for Stephen, in Hale's ire and in Stephen's subsequent skewering. But the outcome was almost grimmer for Persephone. Hale cornered her that night, in their own home, spewing hate and invective, and then he hissed at her that he'd never let her go. Never.

So Persephone learned to avoid rousing the chivalry of any visiting male. There was simply no place for heroes in that cold kingdom, and nothing mattered anymore anyway. Only Hale. And he was doing the best he could. Not his fault she kept on making him angry. She would change. She'd do better. Before her, behind her, above her—only Hale. For all of eternity. Her life, her soul, her entire existence would thereafter be in Hale. Her own private penance for mistakes made and for kindnesses unacknowledged.

But then one bright, cold morning, an unlikely visitor appeared at her chamber. "Name's Leslie," he told her, quite charmingly. "I know, I know. That's a female's name. But that's part of the reason I'm traveling."

Persephone momentarily forgot herself and tumbled over the threshold. "I beg your pardon." She knew she shouldn't invite him in but was so flustered by her tumble that she felt she had no choice. "Please." She scuttled aside so he could enter. "I can see that you are a gentleman."

"Am I?" he said, entering. "That may be part of the problem, too."

Persephone was perplexed. Not only at his words, but at his manner. "Yes, a fine Southern gentleman, I do believe." Unlike every other visitor they'd ever entertained, Leslie did not even seem to notice the corpses stacked high against the wall.

"Lovely abode," said Leslie.

Persephone wondered what he was seeing. "Thank you," she said, then added, "You must know my husband? Hale?"

"Must I?" said Leslie. He moved in closer and whispered words that sounded like a song. "*I fell because of wisdom, but was not destroyed: through her I dived into the great sea, and in those depths I seized a wealth-bestowing pearl.*"

Persephone felt something relax and realign itself within her structure. She almost laughed. She saw something like springtime reflected in the shiny red of Leslie's elytra. Perhaps she could talk to him. Perhaps he would listen.

"The Queen of Sheba wrote that," Leslie explained. "Thousands of years ago."

Persephone didn't understand, and feared she might tumble again, but just then Hale burst into the chamber, dragging a half-drained cockroach corpse behind him.

"Help me with this," he snapped, before he saw their visitor. "And who the hell are you," he said to Leslie. He shot an angry glare at Persephone.

Leslie stepped in immediately to help Hale drag his burden into the living chamber. "Wow," said Leslie. "That's a beauty."

Hale stopped, slid his gaze over every rounded millimeter of their guest. "What the hell does a prissy little ladybug like you know about cockroaches?"

"Nothing," said Leslie, cheerfully. "I don't know much about anything, as a matter of fact. I have so much to learn." He looked from Hale, to Persephone, and back again to Hale. "Will you be my mentor?" Then he spoke in his song voice again. "*I climbed the rope to the boat of understanding.*"

Hale laughed. Persephone felt a terrible urge to tumble. She willed herself to freeze. She never knew how Hale would react to outsiders. And it would have pained her deeply to have had to stack Leslie's shiny red corpse up on top of the cockroach's black one.

But Hale surprised her. "Stay with us," Hale said. His eyes were bright and glinty. "There's a lot I can teach you."

So Leslie stayed. And Persephone was surprised again to see Leslie's still-living bugness follow Hale out the front entry the next morning. She was a little disappointed, too—not that he was living, but just that he was leaving. She was hoping he might stay and shower her with more of his song-words.

Hale and Leslie came back that evening with a plump, still-twitching katydid. Leslie held it still while Hale siphoned off its juices. The night after that, they returned with just a tiny tick. And the night after that, nothing at all. But they entered in high spirits, nonetheless.

"Where'd you go today?" Persephone asked, hoping to elicit a little evening conversation.

"What the hell do you care," Hale shot back.

But Leslie mollified him with a glance. "It was something," Leslie began. "Really something." And he proceeded to tell Persephone about a lake they had visited. And a field of goldenrod. *"I marveled at that light, and grasped it, and brought it up to the sun,"* he sang.

"I want to come with you!" Persephone said, without thinking.

"You'll go where I tell you to go," growled Hale.

"Lighten up," Leslie said to Hale. Persephone waited for the explosion, but it didn't come. If anything, Hale seemed pacified by Leslie's laid-back attitude. Persephone started to tumble in confusion, but stopped herself. A clod of dirt fell suddenly from their ceiling, nearly hitting her. "You okay?" Leslie asked, though his eyes were still on Hale.

A sliver of moonlight slid in through the crack. She was okay. Just a little dazed by the changes in Hale since Leslie appeared. What was going on?

The next morning, she asked again if she could go with them to see the sky and the lake and the field of goldenrod. She braced herself for the worst from Hale, but he didn't even answer. Instead, he nodded to Leslie who took it upon himself to explain to Persephone, in a condescending—no, worse than condescending—in a cruel and prickly voice that had lost all of its music, why that wouldn't be a good idea.

So she stayed alone, again, in the dark chamber. From time to time, she glanced up at the sliver of sunlight that shone in through the crack in the ceiling. *I marveled at that light,* sang in her thoughts. She fell to the task of tidying corpses with more nervous energy than usual; she was thinking, inexplicably, about springtime and flowers and freedom. She realized, suddenly, that while daydreaming she had been stacking the corpses in a pyramid formation. She climbed up and looked around. A dozen more and she would reach the sunlight. Almost. She caught a faint whiff of fennel and tumbled down (it was just quicker that way) to carry up more cadavers. Then she stretched to scratch at the crack in the ceiling with the hard elytra of a dead carrion beetle. The opening sun warmed her senses and reactivated her survival instincts. She dragged up three more cadavers—miraculous strength!—then three more. She kept scratching at the crack until the blueness of the sky startled her to clarity. There was life out there. She smelled it in the air. Dan? Mother? And then she remembered—she could fly! She could do that, and Hale couldn't. He wouldn't be able to catch her. He wouldn't be able to find her. Probably wouldn't even miss her, if her instincts were correct about his relationship with Leslie. Yes. That was it. She saw it quite clearly then. Leslie and Hale. And Leslie no kinder than her husband. Just better at hiding his ugliness behind his poetry-spouting, flattery-spewing, ladybug façade. She had *climbed that rope to the boat of understanding*. Good riddance, boys. You deserve each other. She wished them every happiness that cruelty could engender. Was it happiness they wanted? No matter—as long as she was far, far away when they got it.

New thoughts, ideas, feelings flew in to Persephone from the crack in the mud. She scraped at the edges until the opening was the size of a small tumbling flower beetle. Which is what she was, Persephone reminded herself. She wasn't an assassin bug. She didn't belong there. She could fit through that hole. She could fly away. In her excitement, Persephone started to tumble back down the pyramid of corpses, down, down, back into her life in Hale. But she righted herself, kept her sights on the sky. She kept climbing, fighting down her instinct to tumble. She *fell because of wisdom, but was not destroyed*. She was glad she'd had to train herself—she would not tumble down again.

She took off quickly, without regrets. Her wings trembled at the outset, but a fresh gust of possibility carried her upward. Onward. Life. With all its mysteries. The world was blinding-bright at first, but then, what colors she beheld! Persephone gazed down on the golden tops of trees, the silver flicker of the sun on a lake. Mosquito friends were lighting on its surface. No turning back now. No ends in sight. The sky unfolded before her—her own private passageway into a world without limit. She could almost thank Hale—she was feeling that good—for keeping her in a darkness so complete that it opened her eyes, finally, to light. Every light. Joy was her mate now, her motive, her wings. She inhaled the world as she soared up above it. Freedom. Everything was possible. Even courage. Even somersaults. And she could tumble too, she reminded herself, as much as she wanted. Persephone could just go ahead and tumble through that fennel-scented air all the way to heaven.

A Good Mite Is Hard to Find
(A Silly Little Love Song)

Bruno scanned the dappled field without enthusiasm. He guessed he'd been through about a million mites. Just like the song said. He'd love 'em and he'd leave 'em alone. He pushed out into a relatively furless region, to get a better look at the prospects. That one, too old. This one, too young. The one over there—she might be . . . maybe. "Behind you," he called. Nope. Not smart enough—too bad—to get out of the way of those angry paws. But that's the way it went sometimes. Sometimes you're the scratcher and sometimes you get scratched.

Still, the old cynicism didn't feel as funny as it used to. Used to be, he'd spring from follicle to follicle, from foreleg to hind leg, from muzzle to teat, to take what he wanted with nary a quiver of conscience. Used to be, he'd never worried about anyone's future, his own least of all. But now some new kind of itch—for something beyond the next Dalmation-blood meal or the next empty coupling—something—was springing up inside him and chewing up his gonopores. But what else could he possibly want? He flipped on his back, made himself savor the soft folds of his host's underbelly. Already he had plenty of freedom, a warm place to sleep, enough food for forever, and his pick of partners. What more could a mite desire?

Etta wondered as she wandered through the dander and the dust, how much longer would it take? You know it don't come easy, her mama always said. Her mama told her too that true love would find a way. But she'd also told her that she'd better shop around. It got confusing sometimes. And over how many more follicles would she have to travel, how much more spotted fur would she have to traverse? How much deeper into this scabrous dermis would she have to burrow before True Love finally appeared?

Love. If it even existed. It was difficult, sometimes, to keep from getting cynical. What's love got to do with it, her best friend, Karly, often sang. And Etta was starting to think that Karly might be right. Perhaps love was just a sweet old fashioned notion or a second-hand emotion, even. Perhaps what she was feeling was purely a physiological need, nothing more.

That's when she saw him. Right next to their host's third nipple. So brave, to let himself be exposed like that on that soft, stretchy patch, without the cover of fur. She felt something flutter inside her. Who was he? And right then, right there, Etta knew that she'd always remember that moment. The first time ever I saw your face, her heart sang, I thought the sun rose in your eyes. He was brutally handsome.

Well that's more like it, Bruno thought, when he saw Etta watching him. She was fatally pretty and had good taste besides. You are so beautiful to me, he whispered. Etta didn't hear him. Her thoughts were swirling in circles. Help me, I think I'm falling . . . in love, too fast. This crazy feeling's got me thinking about my future and worrying about my past.

Bruno stood up, stretched himself, and moved in. "Let's spend the night together," he sang to her. "Now I need you more than ever."

She retreated. Moved behind the skin flap to escape his too-male gaze. I'm in trouble, she thought, 'cause he's a rambler and a gambler and a sweet talking ladies man.

But her retreat only made Bruno want her more. Every little thing she does is magic, he thought. He'd never felt this way before.

Every move she makes just turns me on. Even though my life before was tragic, now I know my love for her goes on. That last part he said out loud.

She stopped. Turned. Peeked out from behind the stretchy flap. "Love?" she said. "I want to know what Love is." She hesitated, but made herself say it all. "I want you to show me," she whispered.

Bruno held out his pedipalps. He was learning. He couldn't chase her or she'd run and he didn't want her to run. He'd take a chance on this one. He'd let her come to him. "And then I fooled around and fell in love," he sang, laughing at himself.

Etta sighed. Something softened inside her then, and almost fell out. "What I'll give you since you've asked," she sang sotto, "is all my time together." She edged bravely forward. Perhaps she could trust him. Perhaps he was The One.

Bruno knew that song. His mother used to sing it to him when he was just a mini-mite. "Taking off the days, one by one. Setting them to breathe in the sun."

Etta couldn't believe her ears. Was this really happening? "This is what I give," she sang, edging closer. "This is what I ask you for." She took that last, terrifying step and stood right beside him at the nipple. "Nothing more." She waited then, eyes lowered, for him to sweep her off her pedipalps and take her, body and soul. He was her destiny, and she was his, and she almost wept with happiness to know that she had found him at last, and that from then on they would be together, forever and ever and . . .

But this time it was Bruno who backed away. Something in the way she moved attracted him like no other lover, yes, but it also made him nervous. Did she think he was some kind of hero or something? Did she really think he was the one-female kind? He had to set her straight. It was only fair. "You say you're looking for someone who's never weak, but always strong, to protect you, and defend you, whether you are right or wrong. Someone who would die for you and more, but it ain't me, babe."

Etta was not deterred. Just like him to be so modest. But he wanted her, she knew, and more importantly, she wanted him too. She'd never, as a matter of fact, wanted anyone or anything quite so much. "Just call me angel of the morning," she sang. "Just touch my cheek before you leave me."

She wasn't getting it. He'd have to be more direct. He nudged her away. "No, no, no, it ain't me babe. It ain't me you're looking for, babe."

"Oh," she said then, looking down. "I see." She ran into the deepest part of the furry forest. Bruno tried to follow her, feeling suddenly as if he might have gone too far, and besides, what in Gub's dappled world was wrong with him anyway? But she only ran faster, and when he got too close she said, "Stop. In the name of Love. Before you break my heart."

So he stopped.

Etta took some comfort in telling Karly, and in feeling the support of Karly's male-bashing rants. But she didn't tell her mother. Because Bruno *had* been her true love, Etta knew. Even if Bruno had been too scared and stupid to admit it to himself. He was her true love and she had lost him. And every time she thought of the way he'd flexed and preened on that starchy surface by their host's third nipple, she'd feel him right there beside her again and even though Karly scolded her that she'd better forget him, Etta knew that she'd had a total eclipse of the heart and would not, in spite of what Etta or her mother or anyone might say, ever forget him.

It was to be a mighty long time before she saw him again. And that was fine with Etta, she finally decided. Gave her time to find herself. Gave her time, more specifically, to reflect deeply on the mysteries and limitations of the world she thought she knew and on her place upon it. Sometimes she felt so small and insignificant, as if her very existence lacked purpose and weight. Other times though, she felt large and expansive, important, as if it were up to her, herself, to unlock the secrets of their universe. She started talking to others—not Karly, who was always too wound up in her own little self to see farther than the black nose of their one own Dalmation, and would not even discuss the possibility of lives and worlds outside their own.

Which seemed increasingly absurd to Etta. It stood to reason that if there were other hosts that looked so similar to their own, then there were probably whole other communities of hosts that simply had not yet wandered into their limited field of vision. There might even be other species of beings, for all they knew, who lived on different types of hosts, or even on wholly different terrains. Perhaps they nourished themselves on something other than blood. Perhaps they communicated in an entirely different way, and perhaps it was only the mites who were so mite-centric as to think that they were the only intelligent beings and that theirs was the only world capable of sustaining life. The possibilities were endless. It might even be that some of those life forms were curious about them too, and might, at that very moment, be wondering, as she was wondering, just how they might one day make contact.

And just because no one in her own little mite community had personally experienced these alternative realities didn't mean that they could not exist and how could any sentient being really turn away from that possibility? Karly's was a very isolationist and bigoted way of thinking, it seemed to Etta. Etta needed some new friends.

And soon enough she found them. First Zenith, and through Zenith, Etta met Parsley and Hardwire and Fremont, and together their words sparked new words, new ideas, new possibilities, that had nothing to do with Bruno at all. Hardwire said that Love was an outworn concept, a pitiful distraction, that spoke to conventional expectations and domestic enslavement and to the clichéd obsessions of an obsolete time. And Etta agreed with him. It felt good to be cynical. It felt cathartic. Cleansing. It felt good to stretch her own mental muscles and to discover in herself something hard and sharp and real that was not dependent on the attentions of a male. The only problem was that there was no music in that revelation. There was no music any more, at all Except for sometimes. And sometimes, in the wee, small hours of the morning, when her cynicism could not warm her, Etta wept for the loss. Music. Love. Bruno. Sometimes, at night, when her cerebellum drifted into misty sleep, Etta's romantic and physiological needs chomped down on her intellectual strivings in such an irrational grip of pain and hurt and longing for Bruno that she could barely breathe.

Bruno regretted his moment of panic. He searched for Etta—followed her over the mucousy nostril, along the sharp top edge of the snout, around the phlemy eyes, in and out of the ears, and once even made the long hard trek down the whole length of the backbone to the tip of the tail. But she wouldn't hear him, wouldn't even turn around. She'd made her choice.

So then he made some new friends of his own. Cleo and Chloe and sometimes even Karly. But they never talked at all. Or if they did, as was sometimes the case with Karly, it was to jeer at how strange Etta had become and why was she hanging out with those crazy Expansionists anyway? It still hurt Bruno to hear Etta's name. Which was odd to him, as they hadn't even shared any blood together. But there was something about that little mite that stuck with him, scratched at him where it counted. And sometimes he would casually ask Karly about Etta just to have an excuse to say her name—partly to punish himself, and partly to make sure that she was still out there somewhere, still okay. And even when Karly spat out "Etta" with sharp teeth in the t's, it still rang in Bruno's ears like music, painful and endless, that pulled him to the edge of a place he couldn't bear to go.

"I think I'm going to be sad," he confided to Karly once. "I think it's today." Karl laughed at him.

He deserved that. He sent her away then, along with Chloe and Cleo, as kindly as he could. No need to be cruel. He'd lost his appetites anyway. All of them. Even for the sweetest blood in the tender crook of his host's back haunches. Nothing was the same anymore, because everywhere he looked, he saw Etta. Oh, how can I forget you, girl, when there is always something there to remind me? I was born to love you, and I will never be free.

Love is just a four-letter word, Hardwire told Etta. Etta tried to believe it, especially when she felt Bruno at her back, following her. Especially when she wanted, more than anything, to just turn around and welcome him back into her life. But she knew what Bruno wanted, and he'd already made it abundantly clear that it wasn't love. Grow up, she told herself. Do something with your life. She wished she could be as rational and as scientific as Hardwire. That would make it so much easier to live.

One day, Hardwire announced to everyone, but to Zenith in particular, that he was going out to do some recon work for the cause. Hardwire and Zenith were an item, but when Hardwire told her that she didn't even flinch, even though she must have known what it meant. That she might lose him. That she might never see him again. But Zenith didn't beg him not to go. Didn't even plead with him, as Etta would have, to reconsider whether or not world expansion was worth risking his life over. She just nodded. Science required sacrifice.

"But are you ready?" Etta asked him. She couldn't help herself. "Do you even know what you are jumping into?"

"Does anyone?" Hardwire said.

He had her there.

Bruno hunkered down in a dark spot and heard it all. If only Etta would see him again. If only she would listen. Turn around, Bright Eyes! He wanted to call to her, but knew he didn't have the right. Every now and then I fall apart. Bruno didn't trust this Hardwire fellow. His head was far too large, for one thing. And he didn't like the way he looked at Etta—all intense and all up in her face. He didn't much care for the way Etta looked at him either—as if he were some kind of a hero. You're looking for love in all the wrong places! He wanted to scream it. Don't you get it? The guy acts all smart and brave and cool, but he is only after one thing. Bruno bit his host again and again, just to keep from feeling so entirely powerless. Yeah, you should know, Bruno, he said to himself. That's why you blew it when you had the chance. He sidled in closer. Forgive me, Etta, he whispered. There is someone walking behind you. Turn around! Look at me!

He sighed. So now he'd become a stalker, on top of everything else. He should just back away. Let her be happy. I wish you love, he whispered, before he retreated to one of the darkest spots in the furry forest.

Etta thought she heard something. She felt a tiny little tug on her heart. Bruno? Zenith was busy helping Hardwire prepare for his journey. "Wait until that other host gets close enough," she was saying. "Don't jump until you smell his blood. Jump high and jump deep into the fur, and whatever you do, don't let yourself be brushed off before you can get down to the follicle." So Zenith did care about him, Etta saw then. She just didn't get all gooey about it, like Etta would have. There were so many kinds of love. Etta wished she were more like Zenith—tougher, more pulled together.

There it was again—that tug on her heart. Bruno? Etta foraged out into the darkest fur and rooted around. Maybe it was the old fear, pricked to new life by Hardwire's impending journey, of losing something before you ever even had it. Maybe it was just the thought of wasting any more precious time. But something wouldn't let her give up. Bruno? Finally, there he was, curled up in the darkest part of the undergrowth. He didn't seem to be moving. Bruno? How strange—the panic she felt made the whole world dark. Bruno? Bruno, are you all right? Speak to me, Bruno!

But it was Hardwire who spoke. "Etta," he said. "I've come to say good-bye."

He looked different; his eyes were all shiny and crazy, and before she knew it, he was on top of her. "Get off!" she shouted. She called for Zenith, but Zenith didn't come. "Parsley!" she shouted then. "Fremont!" They both came charging over, but backed away when they saw what was happening.

"C'mon baby," Hardwire said. "Light my fire."

"Help!" Etta called. "I need somebody. Help! Not just anybody."

Bruno felt her words before he heard them. He roused himself. "Etta? I'm coming!" He bounded over a tall patch of bristly hairs and leapt to her defense, though his femurs were shaky from fasting and underuse. He called on the power of love to give him strength.

He pounced onto Hardwire, pictured himself locked in Etta's grateful embrace. But he couldn't knock him off. He understood then how Hardwire had gotten his name. He'd never known such a tough and wiry mite. Bruno held on like death, but Hardwire just kept going at it—"Mine, mine," Hardwire kept chanting. Bruno bit him, on his tarsus, tibia, patella, femur—anywhere he could get a hold. But it was like biting on bone and still Hardwire kept at it. And to make things worse, Hardwire was laughing now, while Etta moaned. That did it. Bruno dug deep inside and pulled out the best part of himself and with supreme effort seized Hardwire's coxa and ripped him from Etta. Then he flipped him, tried to pry off his sternal plate and almost did it too, until Hardwire caught Bruno by the tritosternum and growled, "Say your prayers."

But that's when Bruno caught sight of Etta, her eyes soft with love and forgiveness. "To love another person is to see the face of Gub," he said to her. And somehow found the strength to shake free of Hardwire's steely hold and go right for his hypostome. Which he did. Severed it cleanly with one bite. And then it was all over.

Bruno lay there then, exhausted and shaking.

Just before he lost consciousness, he saw Etta's beautiful face above him, floating like an angel. "Freedom's just another word for nothing left to lose," he whispered.

Etta cradled him in her pedipalps, and tried to make him rest.

But Bruno kept struggling up to consciousness. I don't want to close my eyes. I don't want to fall asleep because I miss you, girl. And I don't want to miss a thing.

"Heal, my love," Etta said. "I'll be here when you wake. I'll always be here when you wake."

And then Bruno slept. Dreamt, for some reason, of a fantastical world filled with something called turtles. When he finally woke, he woke up completely. Gazed on Etta's loveliness and thought he must have woken up in heaven. "Imagine me and you," he said.

"I do," said Etta.

"I think about you day and night."

"It's only right."

"To think about the girl you love and hold her tight."

So happy together.

Parsley and Fremont muttered words of comfort to Zenith and were gratified to see her recover from her loss so quickly. But more than that, Parsley and Fremont were intrigued by the electric connection they witnessed between Etta and this strange new mite.

"It's like, visceral, or something," Fremont said.

Parsley nodded. She had feelings for Fremont, though she would never have confessed to them while Hardwire was around. "It's, like, magical," she said.

Fremont laughed. "You'd think that people would have had enough of silly love songs. But I look around me and I see it isn't so."

Parsley moved in closer. Fremont was a handsome mite. He smelled like the golden leaves that fell, sometimes, from above. She'd never noticed that before. "Some people want to fill the world with silly love songs. But what's wrong with that, I'd like to know?"

Fremont considered the question carefully. Parsley was changing right before his eyes. She seemed to be glowing, from the inside. He needed to touch her. He needed to know her better. It suddenly seemed like the very most important thing in the world he could do. "Nothing wrong with that at all," he said. He took her trembling pedipalps in his own. "So," he said. "Here we go. Again."

Slug Love: A Sonnet

Go slow, my Love—let's make this last all night—
Delay and linger longer, my dear mate,
For to your satin sole I'll hang on tight
And savor hard my sweet lubricious fate.

Slide, there, across my keel, as you ascend,
Let's lose ourselves in love, our trail silk-glossed!
Dilation means elation when you bend
And slip yourself inside me, passion-tossed.

I feel your feelers twitch, my languid love,
Effusion in reclusion, glabrous slimes
In undulating ribbons from above—
All gossamer and writhing with your rimes.

Our viscous strength, our slippery dreams, entwined—
We are for gastropodic ecstasy designed.

Bad Bugs, Bad Bugs— Whatcha Gonna Do?

This is the city. Los Angeles, California. I'm a cop here. A good one. And I've got stories. Man, do I have stories. We've got some bad bugs here. And I mean baaaad. Sinners. Deadly. They keep me hoppin'. Ha ha. That's a joke. Hoppin—get it? I'm a maggot, in case you didn't notice. So I never hop. Just between us, it's all I can do just to cover my beat and catch the bad guys now and then.

10:03 pm—Headed to MacArthur Park. Got an anonymous tip that something was melting in the dark. Sweet green icing. Everywhere. Flowing down. Suspicious. Called for back up. Gannon, my deputy, meets me there.

Looks like someone left the cake out in the rain, Sergeant Friday.
　　Funny, Gannon. Real funny. But seriously. We've got work to do.
　　M. O.?
　　Same as last night. Hit and fly. A quick pierce, penetration, drop the junk, and off.
　　That's a shame. Motivation?
　　ENVY.
　　Envy?

Mosquitoes see those humans all cozied up on their porch swings, with their full bellies and their smug grins . . .

You know something about envy yourself, do you, Sergeant Friday?

. . . when they, the mosquitoes, have to fight for every meal—alone, hungry, always roaming . . .

Sergeant? You okay?

. . . and then they strike! Hard. How you like *that* little prick? Happy?

Geez. Not easy being a maggot, is it Sarge.

Just trying to get into the mindset of the suspect, Officer Gannon. Envy. And you got something against maggots, Gannon? That's funny, coming from a flea. But hey, I'm not the guy who said size matters. Envy is a sin, Gannon. Leads to bad things. As you should know. Very bad. Nasty things. But we've got a job to do. We've got to nab the perp. That's all.

Which one? Old Rappuccini?

Not Old Rapper. His daughter.

Beatrice?

No. His other daughter. Lilith. You know her, Gannon?

Know of her, Sergeant.

Well, from the reports I'm getting, she's worse than her old man.

Worse? Probably got some bad blood somewhere. Guess that means we'd better hurry. How we gonna catch her?

Interview the usual suspects. Find the tick, number one.

Teddy the Tick?

None other. Fat. GLUTTONOUS. Shouldn't be too hard to find. Booked him just last month, and what does he do, first minute he's out? Burrows in on some poor vertebrate and stuffs himself sick again. Ready to bust, last I saw him. He can't have gotten far.

I'll go find him. And Sarge, why don't you give me those files on Lilith?

What for?

Research. You know—Nymphs? Blood meals? Could be useful.

Thanks, Gannon. But I'll hold onto these for now. What's that? Above us.

What? The bee?

No. The S.O.Bug that just sucked out her sweetness and shot in his venom. Never mind. I know who it was.

Sounds personal.

It is. William the Wasp. One of the most opportunistic parasites you'll ever encounter. Paralyzes his victims then leaves them to die a slow painful death. And for what? To nourish his own entitled offspring, his own ego, that's what. I'd know him anywhere. Those big black eyes, that tiny waist. Looks dapper, William does, but he's GREEDY as they come. There he goes again! Stop! Police!

Don't think he heard you, Sarge.

He heard me. He's questing.

Questing?

Looking for victims.

Well, a bug's got to live.

Yeah, but not that way. Besides, William doesn't do it because he's hungry. He does it because he *can*—because he always wants more, more, more. And because he has no conscience. Point in fact, he invades honeybee nests and steals honey from the broods—like taking candy from babies! And he doesn't care, either. Not so long as he gets what he wants. And he wants *every*thing.

You don't like him much, do you Sarge.

Sneaks up on his victims, gains their trust, then . . . Zap! Takes 'em for all they're worth. Poor slobs never have a chance. No sir. I do not like William the Wasp. Self-entitled bastard. Greed is a terrible thing.

Right, Sarge.

And gluttony is just another kind of greed, when you think of it. So where is Teddy, anyway? Weren't you going after Teddy?

10:20 pm—Hot night. Full moon. In primary pursuit of female mosquito, armed and dangerous. In secondary pursuit of male wasp, disarmingly polite, caught red-probiscussed in the act of immobilizing an innocent by-flyer. Officer Gannon is still, supposedly, rounding up suspects. I remain on the scene, looking for clues. Two snails are sliming up the sidewalk, wasting time.

Is it safe?

Is what safe?

Us. The moon. Out in the open like this. Is it safe?

Safe enough. I'm tired, Lucas.

You're lazy, you mean. Too lazy to save your own membrane.

Lazy? Who you calling lazy? You're so lazy, you fertilize your own eggs.

Yeah, well, so you're so lazy you wait for your food to find you.

Yeah, like you don't. At least I don't just lie back and make my slime move me along.

That's because you're too lazy to have slime.

I have more slime than you do!

Prove it, gastropod!

I will! Uh oh. Look! Shadow overhead! No, really! Run away! Run away!

Run? Me? Too tired.

Too lazy!

Oh yeah? . . .

10:27 pm—Two seagulls eat a sluggish and slippery dinner. Too bad, but Nature exacts her own justice. SLOTH. Another deadly sin. Too bad.

10:31 pm—A pale young termite—wood-boring, I'd say—sets down right beside me. Appears to be agitated. He's going on about something. Chewing on a mulberry leaf. Doesn't see me. Shows signs of intoxication.

Wicked Uncle! There's the rub! You'd do my mother while your own brother lies yet unwept in his grave.

10:32 pm—I smell trouble. Or is that just the mulberry leaf?

Who goes there? Father? Are you the ghost of my father?

No. I'm Sergeant Friday. I'm a cop. And this is the city. Who are you?

My kinsmen call me Hamlet, but I call myself a symbol of Sorrow, a palace of Pain, a fount of Frustration, a wraith of Wrath!

Wherefore doth thou call thyself these things? And wherefore am I speaking like this?

It's addictive. Like so many things.

Lay off the mulberry leaves, son. Do you youngsters know what these goofballs are made of?

I don't care!

Take it easy, son. I can see you're upset.

Upset, hell! I'm going to kill him!

Ah! So you are angry then. (I pause to record this in my notes. ANGER. Might be a lead.)

Angry, yes! That which hath its roots in unspeakable sorrow! Butt out, old man, or I'll gnaw right through your official demeanor, right into your own pain-laden heart!

Right into my what? Say! Are you threatening me? Okay, okay. You're tough, young man. But are you tough enough to do the right thing?

Huh?

The right thing. You heard me. Give up your destructive ways. Go back to your tower. Return to your caste.

But I have been cast out! Are you not listening? By my own uncle, my own mother!

Now we're getting somewhere.

10:40 pm—Young Hamlet is obviously deranged with grief. He will be an unreliable witness, but I have to try. I'm a cop. It's my job.

So, Hamlet. How did it make you feel when your mother did the dirty with your uncle?

(His antennae begin to twitch. I press on.) Did it make you *angry*? Did it make you *hate females*?

No, not all females. But my mother . . .

Exactly. And I bet you'd like to get revenge on females because of that.

Well, maybe, but . . .

In fact, I bet you'd like to see evil females be punished for their actions.

Evil?

Yes, evil. Females who pierce and poison other living beings for no reason . . .

But my mother didn't . . .

For no other reason but their own *envy* of all that is good and decent . . .

My uncle may have poisoned my father, but my mother? No, she . . .

So, you *do* know Lilith?

Who?

Rapuccine's daughter. Come on now, son. We can do this the easy way, or we can do this the hard way.

10:49 pm—Hamlet flies away. Damn. And I was getting so close.

10:59 pm—Officer Gannon returns. Without Teddy the Tick. Instead, one black widow in tow. Female. Luscious. She's a looker, all right. But she's got bad news written all over her.

At ease, Gannon. I've got this. Ma'am?

Her name's Robinson. I brought her in for questioning. I caught her sneaking away from Rappucini's. She knows something.

You're right, Officer Gannon. I do know something. I know a good looking flea when I see him. Mmmmmm. And a maggot with bulges in all the right places.

Ma'am?

Don't let her fool you, Sergeant, with those hoochie-coochie moves and those fancy words. This dame's no good.

Why, Officer Gannon! Whatever do you mean?

Relax, Gannon. The widow and I understand each other. Don't we, ma'am. Go find the tick, Gannon. I got this covered.

11:05 pm—Gannon leaves. Finally. Holy smokes, what a dame.

So. Here's to you, Mrs. Robinson.

You're very gracious, Sergeant Friday. Graceful too. Why don't you come over here. Beside me. A little closer.

Policy, ma'am.

Oh, you big strong males with your silly little policies.

Well, I suppose I could make an exception.

You want to, don't you? Don't you?

Yes ma'am, I do. I really do, but . . . Mrs. Robinson? Are you trying to seduce me?

11:21 pm—Gannon returns. Too soon. Still tick-less.

Watch out for her, Sarge! We don't want any trouble from you, Widow.

Mind your own business, Gannon. I don't mind a reasonable amount of trouble.

Hey, Sarge. You stole that line from Bogie.

11:23 pm—So what if I did? Widow moves in closer. Says she wants to eat me up. I tell her I wouldn't do that if I was her. I resume the interrogation.

So, what's the story, Widow? What's your sin?

My sin?

Don't play coy with me, sister. Everyone's got one.

My sin? You mean, besides killing my husbands and eating my young and paralyzing a human or two?

Yes, ma'am.

PRIDE. I guess. Pride in my powers. Over others, I mean. I've been bad—worse than you could know.

You're taking the fall, Widow. But first, tell me about Lilith.

I won't. She's my friend. I'll never betray her.

Honor among thieves, eh Widow?

Among murderers, Sergeant. Don't delude yourself.

Book her, Gannon. Murder One.

11:33 pm—The widow laughs. A sweet, dark, pretty laugh. Gannon laughs too. Not a pretty sound at all. I've had enough. I'm a cop. A good cop.

Cough it up, Widow. Quit wasting time.

Help me.

You won't need much of anybody's help. You're good.

I deserve that. But the lie was in the way I said it, not at all in what I said. It's my own fault if you can't believe me now.

Ah, now you're dangerous.

11:45 pm—A cockroach—one of those big ugly ones—smears his glance all over the widow as he passes.

Whooeee. She *is fine*.

Stop. Police. Spread 'em.

What for? Okay, okay. What's the charge?

Interfering with an officer in the line of duty.

Say what?

Save it. Name?

Gregor.

Gregor who.

Cockroach. Gregor Von Cockroach. A.k.a. Gregor Samsa. Just trying to cooperate, Officer. Just trying to save you some trouble.

Search him, Officer Gannon.

But he's a . . . ew . . . cockroach.

And you're a cop. Search him.

But what about the widow?

I'll hold on to her.

Sure you will, Sarge.

Sarcasm? This will go in the report.

11:50 pm—I use the widow's own web to tie her up. I can't help noticing that it's made of silk. Soft. Smells like roses. But strong enough. I test it. I hate to see those delicate gams wound up in all that mess, but she crossed the line and I'm a cop. A good one. Still, it's hard to pry my eyes away from the widow, all tied up like that. Believe you me. But I've got a job to do.

So, Von Cockroach, a.k.a. Samsa. What brings you here so late? Returning to the scene of the crime?

What crime?

Cut the crap. We need answers, and you look like a roach in the know.

You got the wrong guy. I was just passing by and I heard this lady . . .

You know her?

Would like to.

11:55 pm—Cockroach is acting suspicious. Jumpy. Shows more than a passing interest in our widow.

I'll ask you one more time, Cockroach. What brings you here so late?

Late? Late for what?

No talking, eh? Take your filthy eyes off the lady. Here, Gannon. Take her.

Gladly.

Not too far.

So, Cockroach. You don't seem to understand that you're being interrogated by an officer of the law.

Sorry. I'm in kind of a hurry.

A hurry? Why's that? What brings you to MacArthur Park anyway? Off the beaten path for you, isn't it, buddy?

Is it?

I ask the questions. You answer. *Capiche*?

Capiche?

That means, "Do you understand?" It's Italian. I get around.

Yeah, Italian. I got that part. It just sounded strange coming from a maggot.

I'm a cop.

Okay, a maggot cop. And yes, I capiche. I'm pickin' up what you're puttin' down. It's just that . . . Can we talk male to male?

Sure. So, what's all the mystery about? Lilith?

Lilith? Who's Lilith? I'm talkin' bout pheromones, man. Pheromones! I'm talking about LUST! I can't help myself. Once I get a whiff of that female sauce I come running. It's a sickness, man. It already got all my brothers and cousins killed dead. I'm at its mercy, Sergeant. Can you help me? Lock me up or something? Save me from myself?

Midnight—LUST. The last deadly sin. Poor 'roach. I almost feel sorry for him. Lust is a hard sin to beat. I know exactly how he . . . Strike that from the report. I'm a cop.

I'll do what I can, Cockroach. You help me, and I'll help you. First, tell me everything you know about Lilith.

Sorry, man. Can't help you there. Who is she? Is she hot?

What? No. I don't know. That's not the point. She's a murderess.

Yeah, that sounds about right.

Don't I know it.

Pheromones get to you too?

Not me. I'm a cop.

Now you're being the dodgy one. C'mon, man. Whole truth and nothing but the truth? You can tell me—I'm clean. In spite of rumors you probably heard. I don't mess with no one's business. Just eat the old stuff that gets left out. I got a bum rap. You know how that goes—prejudice, profiling. You must know what I'm talking about—you're a maggot. Once you get a rep, there's not much you can do.

I don't . . .

C'mon. You can't tell me you don't get a lot of maggot jokes.

Well yes, but . . . Yes. You're right. I hate those maggot jokes. Even my friends laugh about me being a cop. They say it's because I want to be near dead bodies.

That blows, man. I hear ya.

When all I want to do is help make the world a safer place. Is that a crime?

No way! You're doing the world a service! I know just what you mean. I'd like to add something to the world myself. The problem is, well, it's complicated. Has to do with changing forms and making art and metafiction and things that . . . well, anyway, the world needs more bugs like you and me.

Meta . . . who? Whatever. Problem is, the world can't get past our names, our appearance.

Exactly! And it works both ways, too. It's that whole appearance vs. reality trip. Like there's this one really bad dude I know—eats children, tortures females, betrays friends—but because he happens to be ladybug—a *lady* bug for Christ's sake—no one ever suspects him. They think he's *cute!* That guy gets away with murder, first degree.

Those are the hardest ones to catch. Do you have any other info on him that I could . . .

And then, I know this other guy—sweet, loyal, wise, dependable as dirt, at least as intelligent as you and me—but because he's a dung beetle . . .

Don't tell me. I already know what you're going to say. I don't know where folks get these ideas, but there ought to be a law . . .

That's what I'm saying! Prejudice, Sergeant. Pure and simple. If you ask me, prejudice ought to be counted a worse sin than a lot of the others.

Certainly worse than lust.

You got that right.

Hey! Over there! Hate to break up your little tea party, but the widow here is spinning webs again and it's getting late, and don't we have a criminal to catch or something?

Roger, Gannon. Don't get your feelers in a wad. I'm interviewing a witness here. And have you ever heard of insubordination?

Insubord—what? No, I haven't, as a matter of fact. I must not be as smart as you and your roachy friend. Have you ever heard of quitting? Because that's what I'm thinking about doing right now.

Excuse me, Cockroach. I have something to attend to. You're free to go.

I'll stay, if you don't mind. I've enjoyed our little *tête-à-tête*. You're a good maggot, Sergeant Friday.

12:07 am—It's been a long night. Lost a lead, but gained a friend. Ugh. Strike that from the report. Back to work. Not enough evidence to hold the widow, so have to release her on her own recognizance. Especially since Officer Gannon already set her free and then took off himself. That will go on his permanent record. And he never did bring me the tick either. As for Lilith, the mosquitoes are notoriously closed-mouthed. Investigation will have to wait another day.

So, Sergeant, too bad about the widow. She was really ripe.

Yeah. Too bad. But listen. I've got a question for you. Just between you and me—I hear that you roaches eat poison like there's no tomorrow and that the humans can't stop you anymore. I hear that you're going to take over the world.

Well, you're right about the poison. I can't speak for all of us, but I personally find it very tasty. As for being unstoppable, there's still that little lust problem we discussed. And word is, humans are getting wise to that. But honestly—look around you—if we could take over the world, why would we? Humans waste the best parts of it and then leave their shit—just look at it—lying around everywhere. I mean, really. It's a mess. The humans would need to clean it up a lot before we'd want it.

12:15 am—I like the way this guy thinks—he's a bug's bug. Guess Lilith must have packed it in for the night. Time to go home.

Wait a minute, Cockroach. Can I call you Gregor? There's one more thing. Looks like I'm going to need a new partner.

A partner? You mean like a deputy? Would I get to chase widows? And ladybug buggers?

Interested?

Interested? Damn straight I'm interested.

1:01 am—Hot night. New day. Time to wrap it up. But it's weird. I'm not tired anymore. Gregor looked at me like . . . like he admired me or something. It choked me up. It really did. Go home, I told him. Come back in the morning, ready to work. Dirty business, being a cop. But together, we just might clean up this city. And then, you know what Gregor said? He said, who knows—we just might do that. He said that this could be a start of a beautiful friendship. And that got me thinking. Yeah, he might be right. That this might be the start of a whole new chapter. A book maybe. Maybe even a movie deal. Yeah. A movie deal. I like the sound of that. And why not? This is the city. Los Angeles, California. Anything can happen.

Metamorphosis

Every day, something new. It was getting so that Harry was almost afraid of what would come next. First, that confounded hunger gnawing at his insides—day and night, night and day—that kept him always twisting on twigs, palping around for his next leafy mouthful. Needing. Always needing. Embarrassing, is what it was.

And then there was the treachery of his skin—his own skin, shrinking up on him, cracking open, peeling off. And there he'd be. Stripped bare naked in the middle of a meal—two, three, four times. And then, as if that weren't enough, his prolegs—anal and otherwise—had suddenly disappeared. What the hell? And he'd just finally gotten the hang of them too—of how to hook their crocheted rings over bark snags and stem bumps to swing his huge and heavy head (yeah, it was big—got a problem with that?) and crane around, independent of his sausage body, seeking out food, food, must have more food. So what was a caterpillar supposed to do when his claspers all of a sudden unclasped?

That's when Harry had curled up and taken inventory. He counted off his thirteen segments. Check. One spiny horn at the tip of his abdomen. Check. Breathing holes in good working order. Check. But what were these graspy little somethings suddenly wriggling near his mouth? Three pairs of something new, but what?

And it didn't help either that he couldn't see very well. Six little eyes but not a one of them worth a flip. Still, puny little eyes or not, even Harry could see that the times they were most definitely a-changin'. Something was happening to Harry. Something big.

And it was happening fast. There he was one moonlit night, a burly young caterpillar, fully grown, munching and twisting and eating life with the leaves. And then, bam! Wakes up upside down, suspended in mid-air, his butt stuck hard to the underside of a skinny milkweed branch. Just dangling there. Exposed to all the world. Should he call for help? Humiliating, is what it was. The whole world would be laughing then. Hang on, Harry, he told himself. Whatever you do, don't panic. So then he muscled up his huge and heavy head, slowly, so slowly, up to the branch, to his butt, to find out what the dad-blamed catch was. He saw that something sticky, something fibrous, had oozed out from the branch (or had it oozed out from his very own butt?) and was keeping him stuck tight as a fly to a web. He tugged and jerked at the branch. Nope. He wasn't going anywhere. And the realization burrowed a weevil-sized hole into his confidence where some of his pride leaked away. His body uncurled, his head dropped down low. So. Was this how it was going to end for old Harry?

He gave in to one shameful moment of self-pity, but recovered, quick enough. And then his skin started in peeling off again. Are you kidding me? he said aloud. And his anger made him stronger, larger. But right away then he saw that his anger had tiny holes in it too and that his courage was seeping out, drop by drop. This new feeling—was it fear? Harry didn't know how to hold it; he'd never given in to it before. Not that Harry was a hero. Not even close. But always before, Harry'd been able to wriggle out of the way of danger. Find a leaf or a petal. Or the cover of darkness. But now he was helpless—dangling there like a berry on a vine, ripe for the picking. And the sky was bright with predators just waiting for their chance.

"Help me," he prayed. It was an involuntary prayer—he would have stopped it if he could have. But he couldn't stop anything anymore. It was as if something—someone else—was in charge of his life. Though he couldn't see anyone at all—not with those six useless little eyes of his. "Don't leave me here like this," he said to no one. "I need protection. Armor, maybe. Is that too much too ask?"

It wasn't, apparently, because no sooner did Harry ask than something very like armor—thick and tough—started growing on his butt. And it kept on growing too—over his hindermost segment, then down to the next, then the next. And it was kind of pretty, actually, from what Harry could make out with his six little eyes. Silver white, and studded with gold flecks. A helluva miracle, is what it was. "Thank you," Harry said, in case anyone was listening. He was grateful, he really was. And ashamed too, that his requests might have sounded like demands, or worse—like whining.

"You're welcome," a voice said from below.

Harry froze. Not a leaf, not a petal, to cover his nakedness. His only chance was to be very still, very quiet. Try to fade into the scenery.

"Name's Gregor," said the voice. "And I was just messin' with you—sorry. I didn't really do a thing. I'm on a case—undercover— not at liberty to discuss it. But I was passing by and couldn't help noticing that you seem to be . . . in something of a predicament."

Harry tried to crane his head around. "Ya think?" he said.

"Now, don't get testy. It's not true what they say about cockroaches, you know."

"Why should I give a flying flip what anyone says about . . . what? I don't care. I am, as you said, in something of a . . . pre . . . a fix. Can you get me down from here?"

"Whooee! Ride 'em, cowboy!" sang a low-flying mosquito as she passed.

Harry wanted to disappear.

"Hey! That might have been her!" Gregor shouted.

"Might have been who?"

"Her! Lilith! Hey Lilith! Wait up!"

"What?"

"Can't tell you. Sorry." Gregor started pacing. "Shoot," he said. "My very first assignment. And I blew it already. Sorry, man. Gotta run."

"Okay, Greg. Okay." Harry noticed that the silver armor was starting to cover up his spiracles. It was getting hard to breathe. "But before you leave, could you help a brother out?"

"Name's Gregor."

"I heard."

"Not Greg."

"Sorry." Harry sighed. "Can you get me down from here?"

"What should I do? Lilith's long gone by now and Sergeant Friday's gonna have my ass." He started turning in circles, then stopped himself. "Too late. Let it go. Anyway, I'm an officer of the law, newly appointed. Perhaps you've have heard of me in my previous incarnation? Gregor Samsa, the salesman? Who woke up one day and was a . . ."

"Why would I care about salesmen? Especially right now, when I . . . I am . . . can't you see? Turning into some kind of a dad-blamed monster and . . ."

"I'm just saying, I know something about metamorphosis."

"Meta what?"

"You don't read much, do you, Harry."

"I'm a Caterpillar, not some dad-blamed bookworm." Who was this dip-wad? "And much as I'd like to hang around and shoot the breeze with you, this thing is spreading way too fast. Little help?"

Gregor scuttled back and forth. "I'm sorry," he said. "I'm afraid I'm not built for it. Don't tell Friday, but I'm really not cut out for cop work—rescues, captures, all that. I'm an observer, first and foremost. Salesmen have to be, or they'd never know where a victim's—I mean, customer's—soft spot was. That's what I'm best at: observing. I'm like a writer, that way. I observe, and I transform my observations into something people want to hear. Not so good at rescues, unfortunately. Not enough altruism in my blood. And, as you can see, I'm not in the best shape. . ."

"Well, no, I can't see much, Greg. Gregor. And whatever happened to 'protect and serve?' And what do you mean by your 'previous incarnation?'"

"It means I've changed, Harry, as you are changing. It means that, in some ways, I am a manifestation of my own creation."

"Oh, okay. And I'm a butternut squash. All I know is, you're out there in the world running around and I'm stuck up here with some kind of creeping crud sealing off my outside and rotting out my insides and you're telling me that there's not a dad-blamed thing you can do to help?"

"Hmmm. Yes. That's pretty much how it is. Though from the look of that coating, I don't think you'll rot. Mummify, maybe. But I will take careful note of every detail of your death. And in this way, I will immortalize you! How's that?"

"That's perfect, Greg. Thanks a bunch."

"The name is . . . never mind. And I see, for instance, that your pouch is very shiny. I can make that metaphorical for you. *The shimmering shroud of death's embrace.* How's that?"

Harry lunged for the cockroach. His branch bent with the movement, then sprang back sharply, left him jiggling in the breeze.

"Try not to fight it so hard," said a different voice. A deeper voice.

"Who are you?" said Harry. Was every bug in the world going to witness his disgrace?

"Oh, that's Old Dan!" said Gregor. "Hi, Dan! Dan might be able to help you. He's wiser than I am. Stronger. And he's very good at cleaning up messes."

Harry's silver armor kept growing. Squeezing. Hardening. It was moving toward his mouth. If this kept on, very soon Harry wouldn't even be able to speak. Or eat. How then would he survive? In the dusky light he thought he saw thick clumps of mud stuck to Dan's beetley legs. "Can you help me, Dan?" He said it very quietly. He didn't really think he could.

"It depends on what you mean by *help,*" said Dan.

Harry groaned.

"Nothing ever really ends or begins," said Dan. "It only changes form."

"What?"

"Have you ever heard of $E=mc^2$? Diapause? Chrysalis? Pupating?"

"What?" Harry could no longer feel his last three segments. Something was dissolving inside him. And it was more than just his will to live. "Am I dying?" he asked Dan.

"Well, that depends on what you mean by *dying*," said Dan.

Perfect. Still, Harry was beginning to think that it might not be so bad. Dying. Easier, maybe, than hanging on in this riddled world, with its constant threats and annoyances, its unsolvable mysteries, its insatiable hungers. To shed your worries with your skin. To simply shrink away from all that suspense—of which beak might one day pick you off, of which thorn might be the one to impale you. To just go ahead and die and be done with it.

"Things change," Dan said. "For everyone."

The armor was creeping up over Harry's ocelli, but he could still make out the dim figures of Gregory and Dan beneath him. Then there was only Dan.

Gregor was suddenly right beside him, on a nearby branch of the milkweed. "I know what you're going through," he whispered. "And I'm here for you, my friend. Lilith can wait. And Dan's right. Every body changes."

And Harry knew from Gregor's scent and his closeness that this was one secret he had never shared with anyone before.

"Believe it or not, took me quite a while to adjust to my . . . new circumstances, as well. I just woke up like this one day. It was a shock, I can tell you." He was slipping on the stem. "Well, that sucks," Harry said. "Clearly, those feet were not made for foliage." But Gregor kept speaking, even as he slipped away. "Don't be afraid!" he shouted. "Step into the light!" And then he fell, all the way to the grass, landed hard on his back.

Harry closed his remaining eyes to the sight of Gregor's black legs twitching, undignified, in the air. He knew that Gregor wouldn't want him to see that. The odor of dung hung hard in the air. When Harry opened his eyes, he saw that Old Dan had righted Gregor. Good. Better. Harry felt an odd comfort in that. And he felt something else—gratitude?—surge up through his feelers. Those two grubby bugs were the closest he'd ever had to real friends. Even if they couldn't help, even if they couldn't save him, Harry felt lucky, just then, to have their company, unexpectedly steadfast in his final minutes on earth—well, swinging there in space. And to think that Gregor had climbed way up there, on those roachy little legs, just to show Harry that he was not alone. It was a kindness Harry would not forget.

But hard on its tail rode a new sadness. Harry was going to lose this blue green yellow world with its smooth young leaves and its supple branches. Why hadn't he appreciated all that when he had it right there in his mandibles? So many times he'd cursed his eyesight, but to lose these sights, these smells, these tastes, entirely? Never again would Harry bore into the sweet orange flesh of a juicy persimmon. Never again would he inch his way up a sunny boulder. Never again would he catch the fresh morning dew in his spikes. If Harry'd only known that that last sweet bite of clover—chewed hurriedly in his endless quest to get more—was going to be his last. He should have looked around more often, puny eyes or not. He should have ventured out on farther limbs. He should have been more grateful. Less selfish. Less hungry. But how could he have known? He couldn't have known, but still. Harry wanted to live. More than anything, Harry wanted to live. There was still so much he wanted to try, to taste, to feel. It went by too quickly, this life. He'd done what he could, but had it been enough? Harry wanted to try again. "One more chance?" he whispered as the armor hardened, encased him inside.

"There's a difference, Harry," Dan called up to him, "between giving up and giving in. Accept," said Old Dan. "Let go of your old life. A different one is coming."

"A better one?"

"Well," said Dan. "That depends on what you mean by *better.*"

But I have never been religious, Harry would have argued, had his mouth not been entombed then too, with everything else. I don't believe in an afterlife. I believe that a bug makes his own heaven, his own hell, right here on earth. And I believe that when it's over, it's over.

Dan's words floated in and around Harry's disintegrating consciousness. "Believe what you want," Dan said. "That won't change the facts."

Harry felt his organs breaking up then, his old sausage self-breaking down, melting into something formless and liquid. Farewell, Harry, he told himself, with just a breath of left-over sadness because something new—some new feeling—was sliding in though the last pinhole of light. Peace. Safety. And Harry didn't know how or why but he felt—no, he *knew*—that some new promise had been cocooned in there with him. And he slept then, enfolded in the darkness, for a minute, or for a week, or perhaps for eternity. And then, something fluttered. Harry wasn't waking up. Not exactly. But something was, and it was bright, and wet, and spindly, and new. And he felt the twitching of a soul—was it his?—rebuilding, unfurling, and he saw a picture, blue and orange, emerging. And he saw then that a future—gold veined and silver studded, more dazzling, more splendid, more lofty and sublime than anything he could have, in his limited little caterpillar mind, ever possibly imagined—was getting ready to take flight.

The Mosquito's Tale

Fair Lilith had been captured, fair and square.
Poor Sergeant Friday fixed her with a stare.
"A hard dame to pin down, you know that, yes?
But soon you'll see it's best just to confess."
"So you keep telling me," Fair Lilith cried.
"But rights I have! I will not be denied!"
"True, silence is your right, as you well know,
But speaking now may help me let you go."
"I know the drill. Don't strain yourself," said she.
"But speak I will. I do love to be free."

Sergeant Friday was getting impatient. "Let's cut the couplet crap now, okay?" He moved in closer, positioned himself directly in front of her compound eyes. "So, you're waiving your rights?"

"I'm not waving anything. Except maybe my antennae at your handsome friend over there."

Sergeant Friday glanced back at Gregor. Figured. Friday and dames had never had what you might call an easy relationship. What was it about maggots that females just didn't go for? Suck it up, Friday. You're a cop. A good one. "Don't waste my time, Lily. Or I'll charge you with 'obstructing justice' on top of everything else."

"Ooooo! I'm so scared," she said. "And the name's Lilith."

"Whatever. Spill it, Lilith."

"No sweat," said Lilith. "I love to spill it. I was named after *her*, you know."

"Who?"

Lilith was tempted to just pith this maggoty worm and be done with it. "The original," she said. Whew.

Lilith was what you might call a habitual offender. She knew it, he knew it, and the minute they released her (though Friday would probably never admit it), she'd be out on the streets, at it again. And although much of her offensiveness might be attributed to her ancestry, a good deal of it was purely Lilith herself. To pierce, to suck, to drink deeply of life's sweetness—all that was natural to Lilith as flying. And if she did spit a bit of the bad juice back into her victims sometimes, was she to be blamed for that? Weren't they asking for it, after all, with their flesh all tender, bared and ready?

"Oh," said Sergeant Friday. "*That* Lilith. You sound like you're proud of that."

And Lilith was smart too. She was not one to hang on too long, her probiscus deep in that sweetness, her penetration complete. Not for her the quick slap for that extra greedy moment of plea-sure—that quick slap that ended everything. She'd seen it happen. She knew. It was an art, really, to gain entry without notice. To slip it in, gently, almost kindly, as if doing them a favor, then to get what she wanted and to slip it out again, just as quickly. Before the awareness, that sharp sting of recognition, the recriminations, the consequences. How many had she left like that? Violated, helpless, slapping their own necks? Infected with something . . . but no mat-ter to Lilith. Hers was not a reflective nature, nor was she prone to dwelling on the past. She'd leave them cursing her to the devil or worse. Lilith had no fear of devils, nor of any kind of afterlife. She would be high in the sky by then, looking down, laughing, soaring, fat and happy. Satisfied.

It was a good life.

"I'm very proud of it," said Lilith.

Sergeant Friday sighed again. He was an exceptionally patient maggot. "Suppose we start, then, from the beginning."

"The very beginning?"

"Why not," said Sergeant Friday. "We got nowhere to go."

"So you want the truth, the whole truth, and nothing but . . ."

"Just the facts, ma'am. And talk to *me*, Missy. Not Gregor over there. He hasn't even been deputized yet."

"Sure thing, Sergeant," said Lilith, pulling her gaze reluctantly back to the maggot. "You want the story Chaucerian style, in heroic couplets?"

"Quit stalling, sister. No heroics. Just give it to me straight."

"As you wish, the prisoner moaned,
Though truth, in prose, will be entombed."

"Lilith . . ."

"Okay, okay. Suck the fun right out of the story. I'll give it to you straight if that's what you really want. I'll give you the facts. And the truth too—no extra charge. You asked for it. Here it is, and from the *very* beginning."

THE MOSQUITO'S TALE

In the beginning, there was only ooze. The ooze sat in a pool of itself, quietly, in the bowels of the earth, for hundreds of thousands of years. But one day—no one knows why—the ooze began to stretch and spread. And then it began to leap. And then, after another hundred thousand years, the leaping, flaming licks of ooze became impatient with the confines of its sedimentary prison and began to percolate up, up, through the fissures and the fault lines of the earth's core until it finally burst through the ocean floor itself, where the molten ooze churned the cool water into a rolling boil. It stirred up the ocean for a hundred thousand years, jumping and splashing into the neighboring rivers, but eventually it became impatient with even these liquid limits. So then it bubbled up to the water's surface, where it exploded into the atmosphere in scalding spits and shooting geysers. Which may have been a mistake for the ooze. Because it lost some of its proverbial steam then, and turned into gases that became largely invisible after the first hundred thousand years of spectacular show. And gradually, the ooze came to be hospitably accepted by the carbon dioxide loving vegetation. Which cooled the jets of the ooze considerably, and tamed it, though in a happy and domestically harmonious (mostly) way.

Which was when, in a bubble of vestigial ooze, the first mosquito rose to the surface of the Euphrates and in a pop, appeared on the face of the earth. "I am Lilith," she said. No one had to name her. She already knew who she was.

Lilith spread her lovely wings then and flew over the hills and dales and sand dunes. She was very large. In those days, the concentration of atmospheric oxygen was much richer and Lilith's tracheal system was exceptionally well developed. As were her powers of perception. Lilith delighted in the colorful cups of nectar that sprung up, it seemed, whenever she needed nourishment. She dove into the scented, blooming cups and fed deeply, greedily. She lapped up the nectar with great passion—the same way she lapped up all the sights, sounds, tastes, and furnishings of her miraculous new home. She decided that all these gifts and wonders deserved names of their own. So Lilith named her green steps "leaves"; her thirst quenchers, "rain"; her thorax-warmer, "sun"; and her cover of darkness, "night." Her food receptacles she called, "flowers." She loved these last gifts best of all. Lilith was supremely independent and well suited to her world. She never hungered or thirsted, nor did she know want of any sort.

Until one day, while soaring over the surface of the Euphrates and gazing, as was her habit, at her own graceful reflection in the water below, she saw a bubble floating up to the surface. Ah, thought Lilith. Something new and delicious for me to eat. She swooped down to see it more clearly. Pop, went the bubble, right before her eyes. She prepared to ingest it, but hesitated when she saw that it looked a lot like her own reflection. Except that it was missing a proboscis. And its antennae were much larger than hers. "Feathery" was the word she created to describe those wondrous antennae. She hovered above the creature, gave it some space. She remembered how disorienting it had been to be thrust so suddenly from a watery world into a dry one. The creature took his time in looking around. Understandably. But he stared right at her without even a flicker of recognition. Oh dear, thought Lilith. Perhaps his ganglia are incompletely connected to his nerve centers. Or perhaps his vision is not yet fully operational. She moved in closer. But just then the flagellum of the creature's antennae brushed up against her own. Lilith's sensilla leapt and flew! She'd never felt anything like that before. "I'll call you 'Adam'," she said to the creature, and just like that a new kind of hunger tugged at Lilith. She savored the touch of his feathery flagellum and moved against it. "Adam, come," said Lilith. Adam obliged. He was educable. She decided to keep him.

Lilith and Adam became inseparable. Literally, for a while there. Lilith marveled each day at her good fortune. Adam was docile and kind and always ready to satisfy her new hunger. She taught him to how to light, carefully, on flowers and how to distinguish the sweet ones from the bitter. She showed him how to avoid the lethal tail slap of the giant footed beasts and how to hide from the giant beaks and great whooshing wings of the enormous creatures that flew above them. "Hide under the leaves," she told him, and very quickly Adam understood that the green steps and platforms could be used for shelter as well. But he had difficulty understanding abstractions and too often took refuge under the most slender and ferny of his choices. "Those are not big enough to cover you," Lilith told him.

"Big?" said Adam. "Enough?"

So Lilith invented a new word to indicate the suitably sized leaves. "Fronds," she told him. "Hide under these fronds."

She taught him other words, too. "Moon," she taught him, when they returned to the banks of the Euphrates where they'd first met. They coupled again, and yet again, over the teeming waters, in the reflected glow of a moon full and fat as a tick. "Your body is a wonderland," Lilith sang. The words floated to her in an unfamiliar cadence from some kind of netherworld—the future? She liked the sound of them in the lilting breeze, though music had not yet, to her knowledge, been invented. Adam looked at her quizzically. He'd never heard such sounds. "Doesn't matter," said Lilith. "This is what matters," she said, indicating his antennae. "Move it like this," she said, demonstrating. Yes. Just like that. "Love," she taught Adam. "You and me forever."

"Love," said Adam.

And then Lilith felt something overpowering and new. Joy. Boundless. Uncontainable. She felt she might explode with joy. "Paradise," she said, gazing at Adam. He seemed to understand her. He loved her too. "Paradise," he echoed.

And they went on like that, blissfully in love, for quite a while, until one green and sunny day when Lilith felt a new kind of urge. Blood was what she wanted. Something was growing inside of her— something foreign, but friendly—and her ooze-born instincts told her that blood was required to feed it. "So this is what this thing is for," she said of her proboscis. She honed in on the exposed neck of a sleeping, cloven-hoofed giant. She slipped her proboscis in, tentatively at first, but when the giant didn't stir, she retracted it and poked it into his haunches as well. Delicious. And so filling. Lilith had the dizzying sensation that she was drinking in this creature's strength along with his blood. Invigorating stuff! Lilith resolved to feed in this way more often. "Much better than nectar," she told Adam, though she felt immediately ashamed for exulting in her discovery when poor Adam was physiologically incapable—no proboscis!—of imbibing in anything else.

But Adam wasn't listening anyway, as it turned out. He was circling Lilith, preparing to mount her again. "Bring it on," said Lilith, feeling even lustier than usual. And it was only afterwards, when Adam was spent and resting quietly by her side, that Lilith explained to him that he was going to be a father soon.

When the night finally arrived for Lilith to deposit their eggs in a raft on the water, she chose their special site on the Euphrates again. "I think they'll be happy here, don't you?" she asked Adam.

The evening was dark and warm, but she could feel his attention wandering. "One more minute, darling," she said. "I'm almost through here." Adam waited, patiently, to watch her deposit the final eggs. He was such an understanding mate. Lilith felt herself expanding again, with love and gratitude.

"Oh, look!" she said then. "A good portend!" Bright, dazzling objects were dancing across the night sky. "Let's call them 'stars'," Lilith said. "And let's call their movements 'shooting'." Adam watched the sky with Lilith. "Oh, Adam," said Lilith. "Are you half as happy as I am? Starting a family in the midst of all this beauty. I think God must be smiling on us now, don't you?"

But Adam didn't answer. It didn't matter; Lilith had accepted the fact that he was just naturally less loquacious than herself. One had to make allowances for one's mate, it appeared. One had to be realistic about such things. But Adam loved Lilith, and deeply—anyone could see that by the way he was just then transfixed by their beautiful raft of eggs. "We made them ourselves," Lilith said, reading his thoughts. "Adam?" No, he wasn't looking at the eggs, apparently. "Adam?" He was looking at a bubble, slowly rising to the surface. It appeared at exactly the same place where Adam had originally emerged. Lilith forgot all about the eggs then and followed his gaze. A sense of inexplicable foreboding chased away all the bliss. Pop, went the bubble. A third mosquito.

"Lilith!" said Adam.

"No Adam," said Lilith. "Just because she has a proboscis like mine doesn't mean she is me. There's such a thing as individuality, you know, even between females."

Lilith studied the new mosquito. She did look a lot like Lilith herself, though perhaps a bit paler, more delicate in the wingspan. Lilith didn't like the way Adam was studying the interloper. What was this new feeling? Anger and fear both mixed up at once? "Quit gaping," she told Adam. "Let's give her a name." But Adam was speechless in his admiration for this new creature. "Let's see," said Lilith, terrified now and trying desperately distract him. "Let's name her for the stars that keeping shooting across the sky. 'Shoot' can be her name. What do you think?" But Adam didn't respond. Just kept staring.

"Shoot," Adam said at last, but he lit up like a star himself when he said it.

Lilith had never seen him like that before. "No," she said. "Not Shoot. That's not a fitting name." She searched the darkening evening for a different word, an emptier word. One more passive and non-descript. Oh, what was happening to her Adam? The evening was closing in around her. Evening. Eve. What the hell. That would do it. "Her name is Eve," said Lilith, in a tone that closed the matter to Adam entirely.

What Lilith didn't notice in her fixation on Adam's fixation on this new mosquito, this Eve, was that this new mosquito, this Eve, gazed at Lilith and Lilith alone. She appeared suddenly at Lilith's side, stroked Lilith's antennae with her own. Strangely, this made Adam's feathery antennae stand rigidly erect in the muggy air.

"Can we take her home?" asked Adam. Lilith looked at her floating raft of nearly children—not yet ready to emerge.

"I guess we'll have to," Lilith said, fighting down her instincts. What else could she do? And maybe this Eve creature might turn out to be useful, once the little ones arrived.

"What are you staring at?" Lilith said to Eve, seeing for the first time the intensity of Eve's gaze. There was something decidedly unsettling about this female.

"Love," said Eve.

What? Had Eve overheard Lilith's words to Adam as she was emerging from the foam like some kind of a Culicidaen Venus de Milo? Was she mocking her? But no, Eve's compound eyes were soft, not mocking. They didn't appear to have enough fire in them to burn another being.

"What do you mean?" Lilith asked, measuring her words carefully and making them unnaturally polite.

"I love you," said Eve, never taking her eyes off Lilith.

Adam flew around in circles. Clearly, he had no problem with this development.

"It's late," said Lilith. She didn't know what else to say. And besides, she didn't care what or whom this Eve creature loved. Lilith loved Adam. Only Adam. And she wasn't about to lose him. Not for anyone.

But Adam kept changing. There were even longer spaces between his responses now and it appeared sometimes as if he reserved his best words—Lilith's words! She gave them to him!—for Eve alone. For Eve. A pale imitation of herself who could do little more than echo Lilith's own utterances.

He's still my same Adam, Lilith told herself. It's just my imagination. He still loves me, more than ever. Why wouldn't he? I am strong, sexy, graceful, loyal. I am the mother of his children. Surely he wouldn't throw away everything we have just for this sweet little slip of nothingness. This gullible, spineless, addle-brained Eve. Whom I named! Whom I allowed to live out of the goodness of my . . . No. He wouldn't. Adam wouldn't. He'll come to his senses soon.

And Lilith marshaled all her strength of conviction to talk herself into believing that things could be as they had been before. Simple. Happy. Easy. She began to answer her own questions when Adam fell silent, and her words fell faster, faster; sometimes they fell right over the edge of a cliff, sometimes they swirled away from her in directions even Lilith couldn't follow. It wasn't Adam's coupling with Eve that she minded. Not the coupling, exactly. Lilith was too highly evolved to allow herself to feel pain over the physical coupling. It was more the way Adam looked at Eve, hung on her, followed her, as he had once followed Lilith.

"She let's me do what I want," Adam explained to Lilith once. "She never wants to be on top."

Lilith flew from him then—couldn't trust herself to speak. She flew at top speed, trying desperately to outrun her feelings. It didn't work. The pain, the betrayal, the stupidity of it all, kept crashing her right back into the thick of it. Adam? With Eve? Lilith was so distracted, in fact, that she nearly became lunch for a winged giantess who swooped down from nowhere. You're comparing her to ME? Lilith's thoughts screamed all the way up to the heavens, all the way back to the ooze. She sliced through the air, blind with fury; she darted and dashed and whirred herself into exhaustion. Only then did she begin to think clearly. She'd return home, she decided at last. She'd give him one more chance. Perhaps he hadn't fully understood the situation. That was possible—more than possible. Lilith and Adam needed to talk. That, Lilith convinced herself, would fix everything.

So, with a calmness that surprised and also frightened her, Lilith returned to their home. Eve, thankfully, was nowhere in sight. "Adam," Lilith said, softly, for she had taken the time to think it all through and to compose, carefully, her thoughts. "Listen to me. You want someone who doesn't want *you*," she said.

It looked for a moment as if Adam hadn't heard her. He held very still and had a strange expression on his face. Was he thinking? He'd never, to her knowledge, done that before.

"Adam," Lilith said again, assuming that she needed to repeat herself. "You want . . ."

Adam whirled on her. "Same as you," he said.

"What?"

"You heard me."

She had. She just couldn't believe it. Lilith felt something drop out of her midgut then. What, Adam? "You mean that you don't want . . ."

"Yes."

A giant frond crackled overhead but Lilith couldn't move. It crashed then, pinned her to the ground. The wide world whirled. No. Adam? This couldn't be happening. It was all Eve's fault. "I'll kill her," said Lilith, crawling out. She couldn't feel her rear legs but she wasn't about to ask *him* for help.

Adam watched her crawl. There was a ruthlessness to his nature that Lilith hadn't seen before. "Kill?" he said. That was a new word for Adam, probably because Lilith had just then created it.

She didn't feel like explaining. Though when his expression returned to its familiar blankness Lilith almost felt a moment's pity. Ruthless or not, he was still no match for Eve, poor thing. She was using him, it was clear, and God only knew how Eve might contrive to destroy him in the future. Lilith took a farewell look around at the lushness of the garden that had been their whole world. She'll destroy this for you too, Lilith wanted to say. But she wouldn't say it. Not now. Adam—or perhaps it was the fall—had punctured something in Lilith's crop that was never going to heal. No, he and Eve deserved each other, and if they led one another right into hell, it was Lilith's business no longer. He'd made that clear.

"Good bye, Adam," said Lilith.

Adam looked at her quizzically. "Good . . . bye?" he said.

Lilith felt something cold and cruel snaking its way through her ganglia. Good, she thought. Make thick my blood. Fill me from tip to top with direst cruelty. Stop up my passage and access to remorse. "Unsex me here," she said to no one.

"Here?" said Adam, as Lilith flew away, her back legs dangling.

Her children, her Lilum, she'd call them, were all that mattered then. They needed no father—the ooze would be their father. "My children," she called. "My darlings, I'm coming!" But when Lilith reached the Euphrates, her raft of offspring were nowhere to be found. "My babies?" she said, searching the surface, and then the river bank, and then, doomed darlings, beneath the water too. Nothing. But from the corner of her compound eye she saw movement—a delicate flutter of movement. "Eve?" she said. "Show yourself!"

Eve emerged then, from the frond that had covered her. She looked different somehow. Plumper, perhaps. And something white and moist was still clinging to her mandibles. "I love you," said Eve. "I can't help myself."

"But Adam . . ." Lilith couldn't bring herself to say, "loves you." No. She wouldn't. "But why are you out here? And where are my babies?"

"I love you," Eve said only. "I want you."

"But . . ."

"And if I can't have you, I'll have your . . ."

Lilith felt herself slipping down the throat of the world. It was swallowing her whole. No. Not her babies. It didn't make any sense. My children? "Monster!" Lilith shrieked, charging Eve with a demonic strength she'd never felt before. "Hell-bitch! Devil!"

But Eve was too fast for her. "I'm telling Adam," Eve said. Her lift-off was miraculously light. Deceptively light. "I'm telling Adam that you killed his children. Because you were so jealous."

Lilith took off after her, but the weight of her grief and her still-useless legs held her down. "My children!" she cried. "I don't understand!"

"Think about it," said Eve, brightly. But then she hovered over Lilith for just one heavy moment. "We could have been happy, you and I," she said before she left.

Lilith couldn't move. She sank back down to the water's edge, touched again and again the surface where her children had been. "Take me too," she said to the ooze. She stayed there for hours, shivering and grieving. But when the moon rose to the top of the darkness, Lilith felt something new stirring within her. It was hate, sharp and potent. But it was more than that too. Blood. She lusted for blood, in a way she hadn't known since, well, since she'd felt her first brood of angels—God rest their innocent souls—stirring within her. Was it possible? Might Adam have impregnated her again, in spite of his fixation on his evil she-cannibal?

Lilith pumped her wings, full of new resolve, and set off to find hot-blooded mammals to feed her new children. She searched a good while, but found at last a whole herd of hairless creatures, sleeping together inside a damp cave. She feasted and gorged herself, consuming hatred with the blood. You shall avenge me, she sang to her new brood, as she fed them with that hot, red, sticky, stolen life-force.

Then she searched the world for a safe place to lay them. She wouldn't go back to the Euphrates—poisoned as it was now with the knowledge of good and evil, and how the one might sometimes hide inside the other. Joy was poisoned for her now. Happiness, impossible. There was only revenge now. And survival. For herself and for her children. She rested one whole night in the West Nile and deposited some of her heaviest babies there, keeping others in reserve. "Go forth and multiply," was her blessing and directive. "I'll be back." And then she flew on, laying broods in the Tigris, the Caspian Sea, the Mediterranean—anywhere she could find a body of water. But she couldn't stay there, she told each brood with a mother's tenderness and with an artist's icy resolve. The waters didn't look right to Lilith—not quite right, not yet. So she kept flying. She would know it when she found it—the perfect spot to establish her queendom—and she couldn't be deterred by maternal tuggings until she did. And anyway, she found herself heavily gifted with perpetual offspring, though she wasn't sure why. It had been quite a while since she'd been with Adam, but there they were, still growing, stretching, weighting down her burgeoning abdomen. She kept flying, searching. "Patience," she told her anxious progeny. "Hang in there for just a little while longer. I'll deposit you soon, I promise."

But just when Lilith was beginning to despair of ever finding the appropriate spot to settle, there it was. A body of dark water, roiling in blood and fury. Perfect. "I'll call you the Red Sea," said Lilith, "and you shall be home to hundreds of thousands of millions of Lilim." And there she laid the last of her children, who grew up and begat their own children, who begat more, and so it continued, for hundreds of thousands of years. But before Lilith's weary carcass lay finally with the weeds in the rushes, she made certain to pass on her bitter wisdom with her genes: "Be as single-minded and as selfish as Adam," she taught them. "Be as ruthless and as conscienceless as Eve. Infect and betray, as we have been infected and betrayed. And for eons we will endure, though thousands of centuries of generations will curse us. But you must laugh, children. Laugh. Because we are the only ones who know the truth."

And at that, the modern Lilith laughed in the stricken faces of Sergeant Friday and Gregor Von Cockroach.

"To keep me here, there's nothing you can do—
"I'm only, to my blood, just being true."
There, Sergeant Friday seemed to lose his fight:
"Though true is true, it surely isn't right."
The cockroach, meanwhile, saw the Sergeant's need.
"I'm grateful, too, to be a different breed."

But Lilith said, "Don't be so smug, my friends.
You suck away lives, too, for 'nobler' ends.
Hypocrisy is the disease you spread—
Your victims are no less reliably dead."
They watched her go—that maggot and that roach,
And felt, anew, the world's ennui encroach.
"What now?" said Greg, his joie-de-vivre lost.
"What else?" said Friday, glumly. "Let's get sauced."

Portrait of the Artist
as a Young Millipede

Dedicated to the memory of
Frank McCourt

Once upon a time and a very good time it was there was a poo-poo bug coming down along the road and this poo-poo bug that was coming down along the road met a nicens little millipede named baby tralala . . .

His father told him that story. So you're moulting again are ye, Stevie, said his father, after.

I am, said baby tralala. Stevie was moulting again. More new legs.

Ay, and what will ye be doing wit all them legs? Ye'll be getting ahead of yerself, is what ye'll be doing.

His father laughed then. So Stevie laughed too. But his feelings were hurt, make no mistake. Why would his own father have laughed?

Ach, and there ye go again. Sensitive as a slithering slug. Stop being sech a sissy, can't ye?

He tried. He did. He would.

Sweet Jaysus, Paddy, sang his mother. And why must ye be tormenting our own good little lad? Saints be praised! He's done nothing wrong. Ach! And now you've gone and made him start moulting all over again, ye have. Good Gub! Little Stevie, can't ye stop it? Do ye have to be shedding yer nasty little self all over my clean nest?

He tried to think what was the right answer to that question. Yes, was probably true. His nasty little self would do what it would do. But no, he told his mother, wisely, I don't. And then the blaspheming stopped and the humming started in again, so he saw then the difference between right and true.

Good Gub. But what is Gub? Stevie wondered, before he remembered that that kind of thinking could lead straight to eternal damnation where his puny little leggies would be set on fire and his thin thorax torched and his abdominal segments doomed to hiss and sizzle forever and ever without burning up because burning up would mean an end to his suffering and Gub never wanted sinners to stop suffering and when he asked himself why would Gub do that to him, a little sissy-pede who never meant anyone any harm, he made himself think about the nicens piece of mossy bark his father brought in for lunch and nothing else because he did not did not did not want to be hurled howling into the abyss and to fry forever which is what would happen if he questioned Gub. Ach.

Stevie kept on moulting, kept on growing new legs. When he counted sixty-four pairs, he decided to leave the nest. Nothing keeping him there, after all. His mother had recently hatched so many new brothers and sisters that he felt himself lost, tossed. But how lovely those words sounded together. Lost and tossed. Tossed and lost. Like two leaves stuck face to face after a good hard rain. Watch yerself around centipedes, said his new friend, Cranly. Centipedes is meaner than Gub. Tch tch! He'll hear ye! But Cranly didn't listen to little Stevie. Cranly wasn't afraid of Gub nor anything else. Except maybe centipedes. They're as like to take a bite out of ye as to look at ye, Cranly said. They eat up our babies ye know. Eat 'em up like berries.

Berries cherries fairies marries. More lovely words. So many to learn. So many to couple up and rearrange and groom and cherish. And a hundred and six pairs of legs now. Fused into your diplosegments, Cranly told him. Cranly was surely the smartest milli Stevie had ever known. But I have more than ye do, Cranly said. And mine are bigger.

Mine thine fine line dine. Pine. What's this then? A lovely female flouncing up the lane. Slender and pale and bathed in the luscious aroma of decaying cantaloupe. She moved in undulating waves, like his, perhaps, but different. Her waves aroused something in young Stephen. Made him twitchy. Itchy. Made him want to climb up on her back and caress her with his legs, his feathery legs, rhythmic, insistent, pulsing. Arch your front segments, he wanted to tell her. Allow me please to entwine myself, to . . .

So ye're finally feeling your gonopods, are ye Dedalus? Nothing wrong with that, said Cranly. Entirely natural for young bucks like ourselves. Relax. Ye've found your sex-legs is all. Don't fight it.

Stephen hated Cranly just then. Why did he have to muck everything up with those kinds of words? It wasn't his gonopods talking. It was love. Pure and, saints be praised, beautiful. The female oscillated her long graceful segments into a wee little opening beneath a slate blue stone. Modest, is what she was. Innocent. And Cranly there helping himself to her fragrance as if he had a right. No! She's not like that! A wild angel she was. A heavenly vision of perfectest loveliness. Mary, he had already named her in his thoughts, after the blessed Virgin herself. Still, there was Cranly, common and profane, soaking up her perfume with his coarseness. For all Stephen knew, he might be wanting to get his feathery feet on her back his own self. Get away with ye! he told Cranly. Get gone! Cranly laughed. But had the female heard Stephen's words as well, mistaken their intent? She slipped quickly out from under the stone and shimmied, with shame it seemed to Stephen, all the way up the hill to a world far away so far, far away. Pride and hope and desire, like crushed herbs in his heart, sent up vapours of maddening incense before the eyes of his mind. Ach. And what's wrong with ye now, said Cranly. Stephen slouched into a glade of freshly cut grass, made himself smell it. The odour so sharp and new it hurt. But he fought his repulsion, made himself inhale its harshness deeply, repeatedly. Gub likes it when we mortify our senses, his mother told him. It is a good odour to breathe. It will calm my heart. It hurt, it mortified. But it was kinder than cantaloupe. It will calm my heart. My heart is quite calm now.

Nothing wrong with me at all, he said to Cranly. Can't you ever leave me be? Like *she did,* he wanted to say, but he wouldn't say that. Truth was, his heart was far from calm. Calm. Balm. If only there were a balm for a heart that had been twisted up and stomped upon, as his had been just then. Would he never see the likes of her again? Gub's will, no doubt. That's what his sainted mother would be sighing. While crying he was inside. Dying, Gub-bless him. Gub's will. If there was a Gub. But what if there weren't? What if there was No One watching, or helping, or punishing? What if he, little spindly legged Stephen Dedalus, was truly all alone on this wide gray earth, with just these rotting leaves, and his smirking friend, and the stink that kept dripping from his own unlovable self—his loathsome corporeal self, his mother called it—oozing from his own traitorous pores, common as dirt? Made in His Own Image? Not bloody likely. Just another lie they'd fed him, along with the mossy bark.

Nothing stirred within his soul but a cold and cruel and loveless lust. His childhood was dead, and with it, his soul's capacity for simple joys, and he was drifting amid life like the barren shell of the moon.

Moon, tune, buffoon, ruin. He tasted the bitterness of the words. Spat them out. Then sucked them back again, savouring the sorrow. Borrow. Tomorrow. What would his tomorrows be like then? Empty as an abandoned nest. If not love, what? If not now, when? How ever would he live out his impassioned dreams? His mighty themes? And then it hit him, like a falling acorn. Beauty. Meaning. He'd make it himself. Art. Artifice. He would live then like his namesake, the great artificer himself. (Even though old Dedalus' well-intentioned invention, while defying convention, was met with contention, and the outcome too bloody to even bear mention.) Ha ha! Rhymes would be his raison d'etre! But not cosily or rosily or easily or breezily. Not teasingly nor pleasingly. No silly rhymes, no. Artful. Serious. Dignified. Gub wouldn't like it if his rhymes gave him too much joy. Tragedy would be more seemly, Stephen decided, particularly for a milli like himself who had known such depths of sorrow already and so recently. Indecently. Stephen pulled himself inward, made himself feel the full import of his epiphany. Art, then, would be his only comfort. His only solace. Alas for poor Stephen Dedalus.

Look to! Cranly shouted. That dove—the very dove of bloody peace—nearly picked you off just then. Where were ye, lad? Lost in your own bloody thoughts again? Well, look to, lad, or ye'll be losing more than that.

Dove. Above. Shove. Love? The words fell into rhythms like waves against the muddy abundance of the riverbed. Bed. Said. Fed. Dead. But he crouched inside the crevice of his most recent revelation—that he would be an Artist. A true Artist. Not like one of those pig-loving, adage-spewing spiders who spin their clichéd, webby wisdom in the corner of a barn and call it Art and then get books written about them. Animated, feature length films. Charlottes and charlatans, all—his was a lonelier, loftier Art. Rhymes were his calling, falling. Failing.

A frog leapt out from the nasturtiums, caught one of Stephen's back segments under his leg, but Stephen wrenched himself free, scurried under the cover of stinging nettle. Safe, for now. But why did life have to be so painful and so perilous? And why did he, a gentle milli, have so many enemies? He was a kind-hearted fellow, without meanness or malice towards any living creature. Well, except for the stupid ones of course, but who in the world could bear them? And the common—he really couldn't suffer them either, but surely he wasn't alone in that feeling? And that female, who had wiled her way into his heart so unscrupulously. A whore is what she was. He hated her. She'd used him.

She toyed with my affections then left me sputtering in the sand, he said to Cranly, with a sob in his voice. Was there ever a milli so misunderstood?

Ach. Cut the crap, Dedalus. You're a flaming drama queen is what ye are. Ye're the only one with worries, are ye? Or is it just that your worries are more important than mine, than his—that cracked snail over there, slipping into nothingness, fighting just to hold himself together? If ye must keep yer head up yer own arse-hole—ye freakin' coprophagist—at least take a glance around ye first. Hear that? That's the song of crickets calling for their mates. Pretty, isn't it? And that smell there, that's the grand and gracious scent of decomposing pears. A true treat for the senses, am I right? But there ye are, pouting around like ye're the centre of the whole bloody tragic universe and the rest of us, bit actors—no, lower than that—we're just the backdrop for your sadness-soaked soliloquies. Fodder for your fulmination. Hear that? I've got something of the gift for gab myself, but ye don't see me flauntin' it around like I'm some sort of a gub-blessed gift to millipedes, do ye?

Stephen had never noticed before how limited his friend was. How pedestrian, really. Predictable. And what was it his father had said? "When you kick out for yourself, Stephen—as I daresay you will one of these days—remember, whatever you do, to mix with gentlemen, fellows of the right kidney."

Stephen started to crawl away. He would not lower himself—at least, not any lower than he had to be, crawling as he was—to dignify such utterances with a response. Bug off, he whispered, too quietly to be heard or so he thought, but then Cranly was suddenly right beside him, his speech low and moist and scratched up with emotion. What would ye do, Stephen Dedalus, if a bloody centipede sank his poisoned fangs into me right here, on this very spot? What would ye do? Rush over to help out yer old friend? Or stand off to the side, making rhymes about my writhing—being, as always, the gub-damned bloody Gub of Creation, always within or behind or beyond the rest of us, invisible, refined out of existence, indifferent, polishing your detritus?

Stephen had to think about that. He really didn't know. He feared that the right answer might not be, once again, the true one. Cranly's bands were changing color. From green to blue. From seen to new. From clean to true. Fascinating. Stephen's rhymes were becoming more complex. More subtle. Saints be praised.

Are ye really honoring the world by separating yerself from it, Stevie?

Separating, deprecating, capitulating, decapitating.

Are ye listening to me at all?

Listening while glistening and christening my thoughts. The rhythm now is changing, yes. More feet. More feet! Iamb I am!

Ach. I give up on ye, lad. Ye really are an arsehole.

Arsehole? Maybe. But he couldn't turn back then. Not for him the suffocated anger of the conformist. He tried to explain it to Cranly. This was the call of life to his soul not the dull gross voice of the world of duties and despair.

Stevie, my friend, do ye know what ye are saying?

Aye. I do. At last. I am destined to learn my own wisdom apart from others. I will forge anew out of the sluggish matter of the earth a new soaring impalpable imperishable being! Just think of it, Cranly! Cranly? Stephen paused and, though his companion did not speak, felt that his words had called up around them a thought-enchanted silence. I am, will be, an Artist, Cranly! An Artist!

Ach, said Cranly. I see that yer set on yer path, I do, lad. Well, good luck to ye then. An artist, full blown. Gub save us all. So I'll be taking my leave. Ye won't be needing the dull gross voice of the world any longer.

Your choice. Your voice. Rejoice!

Ye are an artist indeed. Gub help ye.

A Day in September

The Fire Ants had been shat upon—subtly, covertly, and for centuries. But no more. They would bite now, and with barbed mandibles, and they'd pivot in circles and they'd bite and they'd bite and their venom would burn, burn, blister, burn, and then the others would listen. Then they'd all pay attention.

Their plan of attack had been months in the making. It would involve stealth. Subterfuge. Secrecy—above all, secrecy. To infiltrate the Harvesters themselves—it had never been done before and, well, it would be difficult. But the Fire Ants were prepared. There could be no turning back. Lives would be sacrificed, yes, many lives. But the enemy would be humiliated, as they themselves had been humiliated. And that was worth anything. Everything.

They'd garnered their forces—spent long and arduous hours augmenting their mound densities; constructing underground galleries to house provisions and to screen their silent entry; grooming soldiers to guard every point of access; preparing individuals for their requisite suicides. Their individuals had been well trained. They were ready.

The Harvester Ants suspected nothing. They'd been busy clearing their fields, building their mounds, consuming one species of seed to extinction, then another, swarming and mating, tending their eggs, expanding their own personal nests, as was the right, indeed the duty, of a Harvester Ant in a free market economy. How could they know that on this day—so like every other—their lives would be changed forever?

Jeb had just begun another day of dragging dead leaves to their compound; Nettie was busily tending the eggs; one larvae, Kendra, was just then emerging into her new ant body when the hits—three at once and from three different fronts—ripped holes into everything they'd heretofore seen as inviolable. The armies of crazed Fire Ants blazed through the tunnels, exploded into the nursery, obliterated the larvae chambers. Onlookers stood in mute disbelief. "It isn't real," one of them said. "This didn't happen." Then the outrage set in. "On our soil? To our innocent civilians?"

Miraculously, the Harvester Queen had not been harmed. Her soldiers had pushed her down, down, into the lowest chamber at the first sniff of danger. Wrong or right, dim or bright, she was their Queen and they would protect her to the death. "Make no mistake," she would later declare to her stricken subjects, after just the briefest briefing and a modicum of coaching, "the Harvesters will hunt down and punish those responsible for these cowardly acts."

But who was responsible? How would they find them? Once the dust cleared and the shock of their losses slid into a nearly unbearable sorrow, the Queen left it to one of her top advisors, Snarl Jove, to address the crowds. He faced them with a practiced sincerity, then sharpened their grief and fear to a lethal point. He confided in them about the "new and specific" information they'd just gained from Intelligence sources. Weapons of mass destruction had been found, it appeared, in the Fire Ants homeland, and though he couldn't say more about that, for obvious security reasons, he urged the Harvesters to act boldly, quickly—else they might never again know safety. He advised them also that for their own security, and effective immediately, the Queen had ordered the closure of every mound opening and tunnel.

Only a few blanched at that news. Others, pumped full of urgency and righteous indignation, stepped forward. "We want to help you fight," said many. "We want to rescue the victims," said others. "We want to donate our stores of seeds and honeydew," said the rest.

Snarl Jove was very pleased, and he quickly dispatched some workers to inform the Queen. She sent up her praises to the volunteers. The messenger relayed her words: "Today, our nation saw evil, the very worst in formicidae, and we responded with the best of the Harvesters, with the daring of our rescue workers, with the caring for strangers, and neighbors who came to help in any way they could." The listeners were touched; they drummed their antennae on one another's heads with enthusiasm.

"We want to help too," said a group of ants who'd just happened on the scene and who looked suspiciously like Fire Ants themselves, except that their heads were exceptionally large. Some of them, the ones with absurdly long legs and antennae, ran around erratically. They all appeared to be extremely passionate about wanting to be of assistance to the Harvesters.

Suspicious Harvester citizenry closed in around them.

"Hold on," said Mr. Jove. "These individuals may be useful to us." He had been out in the world long enough to recognize them as ants from the Bigheaded and the Crazy Ant mounds. They'd earned reputations as cunning and unpredictable fighters. He'd heard too that they bore a personal hatred toward the Fire Ants, and had even been known to carry away Fire Ant queens. There might be a way to use them to the Harvester's advantage. "Give them a chance," he said to the good but understandably wary citizens. "We've lost so much already. Let's not lose our trust in others as well."

The ants milled around and chewed on that, but many continued to regard the newcomers with distrust. They were smaller, darker, than the Harvesters. There was something sneaky about the way they moved. Why should they trust them? After all, look what their own celebrated tolerance for outsiders had brought them.

But Jove appeared to have everything under control. "Somebody get them some cherry sap," he said to the Harvesters. "They're our guests." The more liberal-minded Harvesters found solace in this evidence of their leader's compassion. Less generous souls, however, called it a waste of good sap.

Meanwhile, at the Fire Ant colony, there was great rejoicing. The leader, known to many by his code name, "The Contractor," raised his voice to praise his god and his followers. "You have done well, my children," he said. "You have saved the world." He walked in their midst, permitted his followers to be uncharacteristically close to his physical self. "Some may think us cruel," he explained, "but God himself has ordered us to purify our land of all non-believers." He paused dramatically. "This we have begun," he said. "And this we will accomplish!" He nodded to the Fire Ants. They went wild with joy.

The Harvester Queen conferred again with her advisors. "The Weaver Ants said they'd do what they could," reported Secretary Beersfeld, "but their own supplies are low. They volunteered to build silk nests for the wounded, however. And to lend us all the formic acid they could spare."

"Very good, " said the Queen. "Who else will unite with us in our resolve for justice and peace?"

Here the Secretary of Defense shook his head. "Very few," he said. "It's disappointing."

The Queen weighed Beersfeld's words, and sat very still before she spoke. "After all we've done for them?" she said.

He nodded.

"Even the Acacias?" The Acacias were an influential group who had often, in the past, turned to the Harvesters for help.

Beersfeld shook his head. "They called us 'barbaric,'" he reported. "And besides, they have everything they need now. They started up a whole symbiotic relationship with the acacia trees and now they are—as they were so anxious to throw in our faces—completely self-sufficient."

The Queen sighed a long sigh. She hadn't laid a single egg in well over eight hours and her body felt suddenly, unspeakably old. She'd never had many ideas of her own, even during the best of times, and this day had been, well, really confusing. But then one more idea made an appearance. "Ant Lions!" she said, alive again. "They're skilled in guerilla warfare—they know how to lay traps for the enemy." The queen congratulated herself. That would show all those naysayers who'd long regarded her as merely a token queen, a stupid pawn for others to move at their will. That would give them something to think about. It really was a new and wonderful hope. "We'll fight fire with fire, as they say!"

Beersfeld studied his own tarsomeres. "No," he said, quietly. "The Ant Lions have publicly proclaimed that we got what we deserved. They said that other mounds have lived with the fear of annihilation forever, and that it was high time we understood what the ubiquitous threat of violence felt like."

"Well," said the Queen then, sinking deeply into her massive self. "Well." Her intellect was just slightly less limited than was her understanding of her own limitations. But that evening, on the advice of Jove, she agreed to go up to the surface. She would speak to the Harvesters herself. But to avoid any possible embarrassment, she agreed also to mouth only that which her advisors had fed her.

"Good evening," she began, when her subjects quieted. It surprised her, really, how quickly they'd quieted. And they were looking up at her as if they thought she had the answer or something. Well, she did. She did have the answer. And she could remember it too. "Today, our way of life and our very freedom came under attack in a series of deliberate and deadly terrorist acts. The atrocities committed filled us with disbelief, terrible sadness, and a quiet, unyielding anger."

"Send the ants from Hell back to it!" shouted one young male, and others shouted their agreement.

The Queen waited. Jove touched her antenna fleetingly. The subjects were responding exactly the way they needed them to. The Queen paused, waited for their outrage to build into a murderous desire for revenge. Jove mumbled "Perfect" at her back and she brightened at the praise. She continued with what she hoped would seem to be renewed fervor, but what was actually her own secret exultation. They were listening to her! Really listening, for perhaps the first time. No longer, it seemed, would she have to endure the barely suppressed contempt of her own subjects, the derisive jokes made at her expense. She was, it would appear, eloquent. Forceful. Decisive. And it was all because of the Fire Ants. How grateful she felt to their enemies! "The Harvesters were targeted for attack because we're the brightest beacon for freedom and opportunity in the world. And no one will keep that light from shining." She paused for their cheers. Snarl Jove and Secretary Beersfeld moved in beside her, lent their reassuring military presence to her words. It couldn't have been more perfectly timed, more perfectly choreographed, if they themselves had been leading the charge of the Fire Ants. Ignorant barbarians. If only they knew what they'd done. Beersfeld and Jove edged in closer; they told the queen with their antennae to go on, continue, for the good of the Harvesters, they told her, and even though she tasted the sarcasm in their vibrations, she did go on. She would go on. War was what she wanted. War was what they needed. She'd outline the plan and she'd make them like it. She wouldn't be stopped now. Not again. Not ever again. The Queen pressed her tarsi together, artfully, to give the appearance of thoughtfulness.

"None of us," she continued, with a passion that inflamed them all, "will forget this day. Yet we will go forward to defend freedom and all that is good and just in our world."

The response was thunderous. Loud enough, in fact, to largely drown out the cacophony of private thoughts that were just then echoing through the crowd. But what, exactly, are you saying, some of them asked. And how can you tell us those Bigheads and Crazy Ants are our friends, and then tell us that the Atta Ants are our enemies? And why should we declare war on the Atta Ants when it was the Fire Ants who attacked us? A few of the Harvesters actually whispered their concerns. One of them, Jerry, questioned aloud the wisdom of a pre-emptive strike. But he had never really supported the Queen and everyone knew it. He was quickly shouted down. "Coward!" one of his neighbors called him. "Traitor!" Most of his neighbors—already torn by their own doubts and fears and questions—just stepped away from Jerry and gave him his space. It was a dangerous time to be aligned with dissenters. No one knew whom to trust. But Mona whispered to Jerry, before she tiptoed into a denser part of the mob, "Don't worry. We're attacking because the Fire Ants and the Attas are all part of the same *clade*." But she wasn't convinced either. How many more of our young will be sacrificed? she would have asked it if she'd dared. And what will the rest of the world think of us if we stoop to the level of the Fire Ants?

But she didn't dare ask. No one did. To raise questions now, at this emotional juncture, would have been inappropriate, unseemly. Worse, it might have been seen as being unpatriotic. Which they weren't. The Harvesters loved their colony, loved the principles upon which it had been founded. And besides that, they had to believe their Queen. They had no choice.

Each ant looked around and each ant concluded that he, alone, was the only one who had doubts. That everyone else believed in the Queen. Trusted her. Keep it to yourself, each ant told himself. Now is not the time for cynicism. Now is the time to unite. To support. There would be wounded to heal. Fighters to cheer. Grieving families that should not be made to grieve alone. The Harvesters cheered with all of their might. They had to. And not one of them—they'd telegraphed their mutual agreement on this issue through their quivering antennae—not one of them would say out loud what they were really thinking: Go forward, where? And to what? Every truth that had once seemed self-evident was now slippery as sand. They wanted to ask but they wouldn't, didn't. There were not words.

The Road to Melville

And I only am escaped alone to tell thee—Job

ONE

Call me Ickishmel. Some years ago—never mind how long precisely—having little or no wood in my hindgut and nothing particular to interest me in my lonely termite nest, I found myself re-examining the damp, drizzly November in my soul, and felt keenly that loitering under the shady lee of yonder warehouses would not suffice. I resolved to bypass the encroaching melancholy by making a visit to my friend, Ethan Allen, to partake of whatever comforts he might proffer.

Look at the crowds of the gazers there, transfixed in their silent reveries. Seeing price tags, and dinner parties, and me not at all. No matter. Better to be left alone with my orphaned thoughts and with my hungers sharp.

Or so I thought.

But who could have foreseen that on that very day, dark and dismal as it was, and amid strife that should have beaten a lesser termite into wallpaper paste, that I was about to embark on the adventure of a lifetime?

It began when I decided to abandon my dark musings and to transform my wooden self into a bon vivant, a gourmand, a connoisseur, if you will, of all the delicious treats that life, in its infinite abundance, serves up for the tasting. Live, Ickishmel! Actualize your desires! I dove in, headfirst, and ingested the entire canon of Ethan's tastiest hardwoods in one big, hedonistic go. I launched forth with an aspen appetizer (I recommend the "quaking"), and followed that up with a sampling of beech, birch, butternut, cherry, elm, hickory, hornbeam, lacewood, laurel, maple (too sweet), oak, olive, pecan, rosewood, teak, walnut (excellent), and willow. Ethan Allen, you are a friend indeed, and I really do like your selection.

But my hungers were still un-sated. Was it hardwood I was after? Or a different kind of nourishment? Too much reflection! That has always been a problem for me. Too many words undigested and spilling out as from an overfilled vessel. I have been told that I pontificate, that I am uncomfortably loquacious, that my verbosity, in fact, weighs down my story like an anchor. I have been told as well that my digressions do more to distract than enlighten. But I ask you, gentle readers: Who amongst you would *not* want to burrow into the dark secrets of a kindred, soul? And my tale *is* a long one, yes. But should my words then not be suitably reflective of that circumstance?

But perhaps I do digress too much. Act, Ickishmel! Follow your path and do not stray again into the land of fruitless rumination. Get to the point: to that fateful moment when you first laid eyes on his shimmering exoskeleton and knew, without knowing why you knew, that the moment your lives intersected nothing would ever again be the same.

But how did that come to pass? Ah, you see? I need first to explain how I got there, before I get there. Because it was my aforementioned binge on those hardwoods that led to a craving for softwoods (for loblolly pine, in particular, with its subtle perfume—just a trembling of it, not too much!) and then my loblolly lust for the tenderest flesh in the entire pine family awakened in me an enormous, almost existential hunger, for fine cedar—white, yellow—as well as for perhaps some nice, warm, flaky redwood, which is what led me to find a Pier One, with all due haste, or die of regret for the road not taken, and which (after fortifying myself for the journey with a few quick mouthfuls of spruce from the tall and tasty ladder I found leaning on a fence) is where I, intent on action, set the gears of destiny in motion that were to lead me straight to the term who was to become my best friend in all the world.

I found him in the clearance section, burrowed into a finely figured footstool of pure African mahogany. It was a breathtaking piece of artistry—tattooed with stripes, ribbons, ripples, curls—of a caliber that reflected highly on its creator. He was black as the burls in the wood, and had a short, stub-shaped head. His mandibles were shorter than mine, but sharp as spears. A bit menacing, truth be told. But I could see he was frightened. He'd just plopped out some fresh frass at my approach. Poor fellow.

"This is excellent work," I said, ignoring the frass, trying to set him at ease. "Truly exceptional."

He stepped out, warily, from his hiding place.

"I haven't seen burrowing like this since, well, ever," I said. And it was true. I fancied myself something of an artist. I didn't eat merely to survive (as did so many of my fellow coptotermes), but to taste, to explore, to create something beautiful and timeless out of each one of my feasts. But this stranger's work put mine to shame. The depth of his etching. The careful attention to the subject's natural mottling. The painstaking care he took to showcase the tight knots and the crotches in the grain. His art was not (as mine, I fear, so often was) about showing off a flair for the well-placed arabesque. His was a subtler, more organic, approach.

"Who are you," I said, with genuine wonder. "And where in the world are you from?"

"Quickquick," he said.

"No, no. Take your time. I'm not trying to rush you."

He stepped forward then, proudly. "My name Quickquick. I am Cryptoterm. Winged swarmer." He clicked his mandibles together in a way that showed him to be not only a potentially powerful term but a term of endearment as well. Clearly a noble savage in every way. "I do not know where I be come," he said. "But I live far. Very far."

"Welcome," I said, in my kindest voice. I liked him immediately, but it never hurt to be cautious. Cryptoterms. Seemed to me I remembered something about that genus. Seemed to me it was the cryptoterms who devoured their own wounded compatriots. I clicked my own mandibles as ferociously as I could, but unaccustomed as I was to mounting displays of my own fearsomeness, my actions had quite the opposite effect.

Quickquick laughed. Not unkindly. He invited me into his footstool. And just in time too. Because just then a pair of heavy boots stomped over and would have crushed us into pulverized smears of our former termitelyness if we hadn't just then been hoisted, stool and all, into the air. Too close!

Quickquick laughed again. Apparently my skittishness amused him.

Next thing we knew, we were jostling around on some moving conveyance that smelled like patchouli and rattan and musty curtains. It was dark in the conveyance, and warm. Quite comfortable, really. Plenty of good mahogany to satisfy our corporeal hungers, and each other's good company to satisfy our spiritual ones. It was a moveable feast, in every way, and one that filled me completely.

Quickquick had lived a fascinating life, complete with gigantic mounds, and dangerous predators, and yes, cannibalism. He told me about the complexity of the structures that he used to call home, with their highly advanced air ducts and ventilation systems for cooling and heating. He told me also about the fungus gardens. His ancestors had been cultivating fungus gardens for millions of years, he told me. And his particular mound, in his particular colony, had the largest garden of them all. Which was a mixed blessing, it turned out, because the size of his colony's garden aroused envy from many of the other Cryptoterms, and this, in turn, brought unwelcome visitors and upheaval, and ultimately Quickquick's expulsion, along with that of his brothers, sisters, friends, parents. Even the king and queen were overthrown by the superior might (though inferior caste) of those rebellious upstarts. So then he found shelter in a neighboring kingdom, at least, until his unbridled lust for a certain young female in that complex brought down the ire of her relatives, and he was driven from that mound too, and worse, shunned by his own family. Which led him to the village of the humans and to this particularly savory footstool—the very one we were currently feasting on, and resting in, and talking about.

My stories paled in comparison to Quickquick's, but I entertained him by recounting my own reversals and recognitions. How once, when newly orphaned, I'd been in such dire straits that I'd been reduced to eating plastic and foam. I finally took a hard look at the pathetic creature I'd become and pulled myself up out of that degradation and into the clean-living term that he saw before him, but it had been a struggle, not without some drama of its own.

And because Quickquick was such a good listener and because we were stuck in that conveyance for such a long, bumpy time, I told him the whole blow by blow story of how books had saved me. There I was, eating shame with the plastic, when all at once I looked up. A bookcase! Aluminum, alas, but filled with something I'd never before encountered. Pages and pages of the most ambrosial food imaginable—supple and juicy and nourishing. I felt myself coming to life at last—I ate the words with the pages— and it was there that I learned about love and betrayal and beauty and adventure. It was all there, miracle of miracles, for the taking. I consumed it all voraciously, in greedy gulps and with indescribable enthusiasm—and every bite made me hungry for more. I ate my way through daunting and awe-inspiring volumes like *War and Peace*, *The Compleat Works of Shakspeer*, and *Paradise Lost*. I blew through *Gone with the Wind*, cantered amid the *Canterbury Tales*, gobbled up *Grapes of Wrath*, slogged through *Ulysses* (that was a mouthful), and finally, on the highest shelf, I found it—the tastiest tome of all, *Moby Dick*.

The only downside to consuming all those words was the unfortunate side-effect that I mentioned earlier—that my hind-gut had no way of digesting all those words, and so they have remained with me ever since. And though I miss no opportunity to expel them in impromptu speeches and in unsolicited verbal ruminations, there's no getting around the fact that the very breadth and depth of my indigestible vocabulary is often a heavy burden and is slowing me, and you, and the story, down. And not always in wholly pleasurable ways.

My apologies.

But my point was, that by the time I'd finished gorging myself on that luscious library, I was on the very top shelf—right next to the highest windows (with their delicious sills of Noble Fir), and well on my way to the ceiling where I discovered the delectable secret of real, honest, untreated wood beams.

And as Gub was my witness, I would never be hungry again.

"Good show," Quickquick said. I think he meant "story." Still, I decided not to tell him about the time after that when I binged on the laminated parquet flooring. A minor slip, and one I am not proud of, but everybody has them, yes? Anti-climactic, I decided. Would ruin the whole effect.

By the time the conveyance finally stopped, we were faint from the heat and the patchouli-scented air, and were getting a little sick of mahogany besides. But our friendship was forged by then—iron-clad and unassailable. I gazed at Quickquick with wonder. What stroke of divine intervention had led me to him? To this? To us? But I was soon startled out of my reverie by the sound of rolling thunder. Then a crash. Fresh light poured into the eaten-out crevasses of our footstool.

"What you want I should do with this crap?" The roughness of that man-voice was a tad unsettling.

"Good Will," shouted the other.

Whew. Good will, I told Quickquick, means that everyone will be kind and generous and we might even score ourselves some fresh cherry.

TWO

We met Folger (the soldier) in the splintered arm of a dusty old couch. It was one of those seventies models with the "Harvest Gold" upholstery.

"I told him we shouldn't do it," Folger said.

Quickquick looked confused.

"You told who that you shouldn't do what?" I asked.

Folger had an oversized black head and a brown body. His snout was pointed and smelled of something that you didn't want to get too close to. Still, he seemed like a wholesome enough fellow and since my own head was conspicuously orange and my body, an oft-derided maggoty-white, who was I to cast aspersions?

"Oh," Folger said, all agitated, "I'm just trying to do my job, trying to protect that crazy old S.O.B., that maniac Captain who . . ."

Quickquick froze, then dropped a couple more pellets.

I blocked the evidence of his frass with my larger postmentum, so he wouldn't be embarrassed. But when I turned and saw what he could see, I almost dropped a couple myself.

In the shadows stood the largest term I'd ever seen. Had to be a Macroterm. I used to think that Macroterms were something our elders made up to keep us in line, but this was one was no parental fabrication. He was twice as big as Folger the soldier, but gaunt and lanky as a mantis. And with gigantic pincers. But his strangest marking was a lightning-white streak that cut through his reddish brown head and zig-zagged down the length of his whole, very long body.

His voice boomed in the darkness. "So now I'm a crazy old S.O.B.? A maniac, am I?"

Folger, to his credit, looked straight at the giant and refused to back down. He spoke very softly. "What you want to do is crazy, sir. Impossible. And besides, you-know-who might be there. Word is, he's always hanging around the White House these days, trying to get in, and you never know what he'll do next. He's a dangerous one, that one is. You know what they say: *Even the strong start flailin' once they meet El Palin*. Really sir, I think that . . ."

"Ye're not here to think, soldier."

We all stood silent. Waiting.

Unseen, a rogue fire-ant snuck up beside the Macroterm, and just that quick, Folger shot something from his snout that sent the beggar flying. The giant didn't flinch, but I was shaking with fear. A fire-ant? Do you know how nasty their stingers can be? Why, one of us could have been stung! One of us could have been killed! I couldn't get over it. And what was the magic weapon that was hidden inside Folger's nasus?

"*That* is what you're here to do," the Macroterm told Folger, meaning the snout-shot. And then he turned to me, looked me up and down. Found me wanting, it would appear. Turned back to Folger. "Afeard of a stinkin' wasp, are ye, soldier? *No sport in sailin' lest ye see El Palin!*" And when he saw us still standing there he said, "What are they?"

To my surprise, it was Quickquick who spoke first.

"We . . ." he began, choosing his words carefully, no doubt intuiting, as I did, that there was danger afoot and . . . , "help . . . ," the sooner we retreated the, "you . . . ," better. Wait. What?

"Are you crazy, Quickquick? We don't even know what he's trying to do. And what if it *is* impossible, like the guard says?"

"I'm a soldier," said Folger.

But Quickquick wasn't listening. He was peering into the bottom of my cowardly soul. Using some kind of voodoo on me, it seemed, because although he did not speak, his thoughts were loud and clear. His antennae quivered out the word: "Adventure." And "Adventure," his exoskeleton rattled in the still and dust-filled air. Even his pheremones telegraphed the word to me: "Adventure!"

I inhaled the spicy scent of the word and then I held it in my heart. Adventure. I tried some fancy voodoo of my own and saw that Quickquick read my thoughts. Time to take action, is it,

Quickquick? Time to stop talking and start doing? You know me so well, my friend. You know precisely how to propel my pasty-white body into acquiescence. "I'm in," I said. All my other words had fled. I was in Quickquick's world then, speaking only Quickquick's language.

Folger grunted and turned away. "Very well, then," he said. "It appears I am outnumbered. In that case, may I present to you, our Captain. Captain Mayhap."

The Captain acknowledged us with his shivery, lightning-streaked gaze.

"And in the morning," Folger continued, his words heavy as lead-based paint, "we will embark together, in pursuit of the—the Great White Wall." He shuddered, regained himself. "Gub help us all."

THREE

I woke up foggy. Too much hemlock in our dinner, I imagine. My pronotum thrubbed with the sound of Captain Mayhap's voice banging into the morning:

"Hast thou seen the White Wall? Wake ye now, and answer! Hast thou seen the White Wall? Wake ye, I say. Or damn yer everlasting soul to Gub!"

I heard Folger scuttle reluctantly across the linoleum. "O Captain. My Captain. It's far too early for blasphemy."

"Bah!"

"Come back to your rest, sir. You'll need all your strength . . ."

"For what! For what, Folger! To sit in this larder and nibble on toothpicks?

"Well, just until . . ."

". . . we die of old age? Is that what you were going to say? I am a Macroterm, Folger. Do you know what that means?"

I heard Folger sigh and resign himself to hearing it again. He really is uncommonly conscientious for a soldier. And a good term, besides. All he wants, I have learned during our long trip to Washington (we hitchhiked in a carton that was bound for the *Capitol,* though we ended up at *Capitol Records,* and found ourselves buried beneath an avalanche of plastic discs), is to serve out his tour of duty and get back to his wife and family. Folger is a Hospitaliterm—the most eusocial of the social termites. He is not and never will be as daring and adventurous as Quickquick, or the Captain, or me.

(It makes me almost giddy to say that. I am a daring adventurer!)

"Blast you, Folger! I am leaving today. And you can join me or you can bloody well mutiny and see what comes of that. Your choice. But I am off to find the Great White Wall and may the devil take the rest of you if you are not beside me!"

Well, that got me up. For although I consider myself a good and patriotic American (albeit with enough French in me to know a fine wood when I taste it) I have also enough Irish Coptoterm superstition in my blattodea blood to wish for no involvement with the devil.

"I'm in!" I called to the Captain. And the words had lost none of their magic.

"See there!" Captain Mayhap said. "There's a stout one to aid me in my duty! Come here, son. I like the cut of your jib. I'm bound to say you're not as lily-livered as you look."

That's right. That's right. I was most assuredly *not* as lily-livered as I looked and I was more than gratified to have my non-lily-liveredness recognized at last. Captain Mayhap, I was learning, might be a monomaniac, but he was also quite perceptive. I scuttled eagerly to his side.

He took a step away.

"Folger!"

And then we were on our way. We were on the second leg of our journey, quite literally, for we were traveling in the table leg of a colonial style dining set, bound, Folger assured us, for the correct Capitol this time. And from there it would be just a sprightly little stroll across Pennsylvania Avenue, then a spirited saunter past the guard house, and after that a scenic perambulation across the White House lawn.

And then there we'd be. At the Great White Wall.

But it was not to be quite that simple. Captain Mayhap had other plans. Not for him the straight and narrow path of least resistance. No, for our good Captain, the danger *was* the joy. He fell to singing an off-tune little shanty that was aimed, it seemed, at making me as uncomfortable as possible. *Ye will feel like bailin' when ye meet El Palin,* he taunted, as he strode on ahead. *There'll be pain and wailin' if we greet El Palin!*

I made the mistake then of interjecting my own concerns. Folger tried to stop me, but I wouldn't listen. Who was this El Palin creature and what was his connection to the White House? And what earthly reason could there be for courting danger unnecessarily?

That just made the Captain worse, of course. *"Twill be a sad unveilin' when we cross El Palin,"* he sang, his feigned regret barely discernible beneath his undisguised pleasure at making me squirm. And no sooner had we safely disembarked at our nation's capitol than Captain Mayhap launched himself, full speed ahead, into crazy.

"How stalwart are yer wings, lad?"

I looked around. Surely the Captain wasn't talking to me. But Folger had already pressed on ahead, scouting around for any sign of El Palin. And Quickquick was resting under a dandelion. Oh dear. Captain Mayhap was definitely talking to me. Wings? I'd always been a ground term myself. A lover of the earth. Son of the soil. A most devoted terraphile. "Wings?"

"Because we're going to fly," he said, chuckling to himself. "Quickest way."

"Quickest way to what?" Death seemed to me the obvious answer and I really wished our clear-headed Folger were there to talk his Captain out of this newest bit of nonsense.

But Quickquick jumped up, bursting with excitement. "Quickquick fly quick," he said.

"But I . . ."

"I help," Quickquick said.

And before I knew it, we were off.

Well, they were. It took my wings some time to unfurl themselves, and even longer to dry out and macho-up to the point of usefulness.

"Ever heard of a fellow named Icarus?" I offered to their fast-departing backs.

Quickquick did a U-turn then and came back to me. Ah Quickquick. Was there ever a braver, more generous term?

"Climb on me," he said. "Your wings will remember. Trust."

Ever heard of gravity? I wanted to say. But I didn't. Instead, I pulled myself up onto Quickquick's sturdy barrel of a back and allowed myself to be lifted up, up, higher than any bookshelf, or ceiling beam. Higher even than that rooftop where I'd found myself that one awful time, in that one dark swarm of despair.

Trust, I told myself. Trust in Quickquick's goodness and in his strong and beautiful wings. After a while, I looked down. Six lanes of speeding traffic shooting down opposing lanes. I closed my eyes. How easy it would be to just let go, let myself fall into the unknown, obliterate my entire existence in a wing-beat, just one wing-beat is all it would take, under just one of those angry, black rubber rollers.

Quickquick was reading my mind. "Trust," he said again. And then he said, "Fly," as he rolled out from under me and left me soaring solo in the air. "Fly!" he said, again, but with a good deal more urgency.

"Fly?" Oh. I flapped my wings, hard. I sank a little. Panicked. But, "Fly," Quickquick called, so I kept flapping and flapping and then I didn't fall. I didn't fall! I flew. I really did. And the air carried me along, just as it did Quickquick and Mayhap, and I thought then how beautiful and miraculous was this world, and this life, and the whole cosmic set-up.

I wanted to keep flying forever. The world lay beneath me like an undulating sea of green. I was part of the sky then, lost in the blue. One with the heavens. Divine. I caught a glimpse then of something gossamer fluttering by my side. An angel's wing, perhaps? It took a moment before I felt myself dipping, felt a strange coolness on my back. The searing pain came after. Then the realization. It hadn't been an angel's wing, but my own. I screamed like a damselfly. "Help!" I called. "Quickquick! My wing!" I felt the other one unmooring then too—ripping from my flesh and catching in the air current. "Quickquick! I am done for!"

He was at my side in a flash and my old fear of Cryptoterms flew in before I could block it—would he eat me now that I was wounded? But he was already beneath me, buoying me up in the battering wind. I was deeply ashamed. I wondered how often had unexamined stereotypes stood in the way of true love? For Quickquick was truly the truest, in every way. I sank into his strength, sobbing by then, frightened beyond my manly control, but fighting the urge to faint and tumble—for what then would his courage have gained him? The air grew warmer, calmer, as we finally descended into the vast field of green.

I heard Captain Mayhap mutter something about what kind of an idiot . . . But, "Nearly capsized that time, eh sailor?" he said to me, with forced jocularity, when we landed. "That's why we check our riggings before we shove off." He looked away as I regained my composure. "Burnin' daylight," he said. "El Palin will be upon us if we don't . . . ," then, "Starboard ho!" He pointed to the right and lost no time in setting out again.

Folger reappeared out of nowhere. Snapped back his pronotum, shot another dose of nasty stuff out of his nasus. Assassin bug, at Mayhap's left. Direct hit. The Captain didn't even notice; he just kept plunging forward. "Sorry," Folger said, to Quickquick and me, about the poison spray. "It's not pretty, I know. But it works."

"It's amazing," I told him. "I've never known another term who could do that."

"Well, you've probably not known a lot of soldiers," Folger said. But real quick he appeared to be embarrassed, as if he had insulted me. "I didn't mean . . ."

"Oh, but you're right," I said. "I haven't known a lot of soldiers. Only one, actually. An old friend of my father's. His jaws were so huge he couldn't feed himself. Had to be fed by the workers, like a juvenile. Poor fellow."

"All hands on deck!" the Captain shouted back, urging us to hasten our steps. *"No time for trailin' if we see El Palin!"*

Folger nodded, ignoring the Captain. "Trophallaxis," he said to me. "Yeah, I've heard of that too. Though, thank Gub, I can still . . . take care of all that myself." He explained to me then that the soldier terms had developed a lot of strange adaptations through the millennia that allowed them to perform their duties at the highest level. There was a way they could actually rupture their own glands if need be, right there (he showed me), beneath the cuticle, in order to release a sticky yellow fluid to entangle unwanted invaders. "It's called Autothysis," he explained. "But a soldier only gets to do that once," he said, with a wry laugh. "So it had better be for a really good reason."

"Ahoy, Folger!" the Captain was getting impatient.

"Aye aye!" Folger called to his Captain. Then he rushed forward to assume his rightful position in his wild Captain's wake.

FOUR

The sun was burning high overhead when we finally saw it—the guard house—in the distance. I was a mess by then—my wing sockets ripped and raw, my pedipalps dragging, my body dehydrated and more famished than I could ever remember—but I wouldn't complain. The rest of them—Mayhap, Folger, even brave little Quickquick—were no doubt suffering just as fully as I, yet they had all generously agreed to forego air transport entirely in deference to my unfortunate "condition." And their collective kindness warmed me even as the reason for it torched me with humiliation. I was beginning to wish I had never come on this ill-fated adventure—but just as quickly, I rebuked myself for such inwardly thoughts. Where would I be had I never found Quickquick in that footstool? Or Folger in his sofa? Or Mayhap on his monomaniacal quest? Probably hunched over in some dank library, nibbling despondently on some of the lesser classics. Or hiding in a bank vault, consuming self-loathing along with the ten dollar bills. Miserable. Alone. Economically sound but spiritually crippled. Would I really trade a physical fullness for that spiritual emptiness that had plagued me until . . . I watched as Quickquick maneuvered his short legs over the tall grass, rolling from side to side to right himself each time an extra-long blade tickled him off-balance. My heart nearly burst. He was unspeakably dear to me. Unbearably dear. How had I ever lived before him? How could I ever possibly endure it if ever anything was to . . .

"Avast, me timbers!" Captain Mayhap held up one sepulchral pedipalp to halt us in our tracks.

Folger flew to his side. "I see them, my Captain," he whispered. "Get down."

"See who?" I asked.

"Say nothing." Folger's command was deadly quiet. "Quickquick. Up here with me. Icki, you take up the stern. Keep an eye on the Captain. Guard him with your life."

That's when the old guy snickered. At me? At the thought of *me* guarding *him*? And I bristled at that snicker, I can tell you. I may have lost my wings but not my pride. Not entirely, anyway. "I beg your pardon," I said. Captain or no Captain, there was no need for rudeness.

"You can beg all you want," old Mayhap sneered. "That's not going to save ye if the cuckoo wasps have their way."

"Wasps? What wasps?"

"Get down, lad! Before they come back here and gaff us both!"

"But why . . . ?"

"Because they be pirates, is what they be. Crazy, coldhearted opportunists. They never miss a chance to steal and plunder. Ruthless cutthroats, every one. But especially that one."

"Which one?"

" H'ain't ye been listening, lad?"

Pirates? Wasps? Cutthroats? "But Quickquick . . . he's out there. What if he . . . ?"

"Steady as she goes, lad. Steady as she goes. Your Quickquick can handle hisself. That's why Folger took him. And so long as *that one* is not on board . . ."

I was going to be sick. "El Palin?" I whispered.

"The worst one of all." Old Mayhap bit off the name, *El Palin,* then drew out his words with gasps and creaks, as if he were relating a ghost-story instead of the truth. "Never see'd him myself, but I heard stories, all right." He was clearly relishing the shivers he'd injected into my overly-sensitive (I'll admit it) sensibilities. "Why, that one is the worst kind of evil. He would just as soon stick you as look at you, and the worst part is, he'd smile the whole time, like he was doing you a favor, when he did it. Why I heard once that he up and quit on his own minions, that he left them to . . ." Mayhap was actually cackling then, so much was he enjoying my discomfort. I tried not to listen. "But buck up, lad. So long as El Palin is not on board, there may still be a chance for us all."

"But . . . but what if he is there?"

Mayhap shrugged. "Chances is slim."

My brow remained knit. "You mean, the chances of our seeing him are slim? Or that our chances of surviving are slim if we see him?" I didn't really expect him to answer. I thought again about Quickquick. About how he might, even then, have fallen into the sadistic clutches of the most ruthlessly self-serving wasp of them all. I moved to charge to his rescue, and would have, and could have, but just then the Captain reminded me of the duty with which Folger had charged me. *Guard him with your life,* he'd said. The Captain, not Quickquick. As if the Captain's life could possibly be worth more. But I was a term of my word. A good term. A brave term. I scanned the sky for incoming wasps. I thought I saw movement on the horizon. I leapt to cover the Captain's body with my own. I could make Quickquick proud of me, at any rate. I could still do that.

"Get your bony carcass off me!" the Captain shouted. He threw me off, then started to run. I ran after him of course, wanting to shield him from harm. But that just made him accelerate his limping gait, which made me even more determined to fulfill my obligations, which made him run even faster, swearing a lot, even screaming a little, at what he wrongly perceived to be my mania, instead of his own. And we continued in this manner until we had both, in record time, traversed a good deal of lawn and then run smack dab into a very large wasp who was just then having his way with a jonquil.

The wasp clearly did not appreciate being disturbed. He turned on us with an icy stare, and no amount of apologies (from me) or curses (from the Captain) would convince him of the accidental nature of our encounter. He was a very large wasp. With a very large stinger. He waved it at us threateningly. If only Folger were nearby, with his secret nose-weapon. I looked around, but it was only the three of us. The Captain, me, and, and . . . "May I inquire as to your name?" I politely interjected.

But he had already dismissed my presence and was circling in on the Captain. I slid my body between them, hoping, I suppose, to create a distraction. "Because I was thinking," I continued, "that perhaps we could help you find your way out of this. This sea of grass, I mean," I said, without having any idea what I would say next, "is so endlessly vast, don't you think? Why you can gaze and gaze but you can't see the edges, and to be lost out here, as my friend and I are clearly not, but which I was thinking that possibly you might be, could be a daunting situation, don't you think? And then, it might be that . . ."

"Palin," he said, still staring down the Captain. "El Palin to you. And this," he said, and no sooner did he say it than a hundred wasps materialized right behind him, "is my . . . well, let's just call them my *entourage*." I think he actually winked at us then.

The Captain looked paler than ever, as if he had not really, until that moment, believed in this legend's existence at all. But he puffed up, my brave Captain did, to twice his normal size, and said to me, "It appears, my lad, that we may have run afoul."

And it did, indeed, appear that way. And it might have been our end had it not been for the fact that this Palin character's arrogance far outweighed his intelligence.

"Don't even think about misunderestimating me," El Palin said.

I swallowed my fear. I wanted to tell him there was no such word, but the welfare of the Captain had been left in my charge and I would not let him down. "Impressive," I said to El Palin, indicating the hordes of angry wasps that were clearly more than ready to do their worst by us. I had to buy some time. Just then, I felt a rumble in the earth that I recognized from the city. A big conveyance, heading our way. Sometimes these conveyances brought paper goods, sometimes flooring, sometimes furniture. But they always brought men. And the men in these particular conveyances smelled of something—purpose? anger? insecticides? I said a silent prayer of thanks for my highly attenuated sense of smell, and then I said to El Palin, calmly as I could, "Too bad your minions are not able to fly. That would be quite a sight."

"Can't fly?" he said. "Of course they can fly!" And with a nod he commanded them to the skies. The effect was breathtaking, I must say. Hundreds of winged creatures, rising up in one coordinated rush, their iridescent wings all glinting in the sun like diamonds. It was all so astonishingly magnificent, in fact, that for a moment I forgot about my plan. But I remembered just in time—as the man-conveyance bumped over the lawn and shot up a spray of golden liquid that entombed the swarm mid-flight. "Run!" I said to Mayhap. I stayed right behind him, shoving him forward when he flagged. "Go leeward!" I shouted, hoping that some nautical jargon might spur him on. It was hard running for an old term, but he did it. We outran the golden shower and we didn't stop running until we felt the cold concrete of the Guard House beneath our pedipalps.

"Whew, that was a close one," I said. Clichéd, but true.

Captain Mayhap took a minute to catch his breath, but then he looked at me with a softness, a sanity, that I hadn't seen before. "Ye did grand, lad. I am beholden to ye."

Well that caught me in the esophagus, I can tell you. I had done it. Me. I had saved the Captain and myself and was just about to respond with something probably disproportionately sappy when a low and oily voice said, "Well, shoot. Isn't that just doggoned special. The wingless wonder saved the crazy old coot. You betcha it's time to celebrate."

El Palin stepped out from behind a tool box. Murder in his eyes.

I shoved the captain off the porch. "Abandon ship!" And then I turned to face my fate. I hoped he'd do it quickly—with just one fast, poison stab, and no dramatic dismemberment or disemboweling beforehand. "I knew you'd fall for it," I said. I couldn't help myself. He was just so stupid.

His expression twisted into something terrifying. He was not going to do it quickly, I saw then. I recounted all the moments of my life leading up to that one—the delicious and the sordid—but I got stuck, again, on that one shiny moment when I found Quickquick in that African mahogany, and then our journey together, and the adventures I'd had since. It was worth it, whatever this monster did to me now. I had no regrets.

"Lay on, Palin," I shouted. "And damned be him that first cries, 'Hold! Enough!'"

And then the scuffle ensued. He had me over a barrel once, but much to my amazement, I turned the tide once or twice before my strength gave out. But finally, he had me, tied and true. He tore off my one dangling wing, then pinned me down and readied his stinger. I closed my eyes. My last thought was of Quickquick. His shining black exoskeleton, his trusting soul, his propensity for dropping frass whenever he became overstimulated. I bade him a fond farewell, thanked him for his loyalty. I could almost smell him, right there beside me.

And then I did smell him. Quickquick? He hurled himself at the evil Palin, and managed to throw the wasp off-balance—at least long enough for him to roll us both off the porch together and into the waiting clover. I looked up, expecting El Palin to leap down on top of us, but saw instead Folger, readying his nasus.

He took his shot. Direct hit. But oddly, the wasp did not fall. He did not even stagger. Folger took another shot. Another hit. Still, nothing. What happened after that seemed to happen in slow motion. Quickquick was pushing me to go, go, but over my shoulder I saw everything—Folger reaching beneath his own cuticle, stabbing himself—the thick, yellow fluid, sticky as sap, dripping onto El Palin's appendages, entangling them, and the more the pirate struggled, the more he was ensnared. Folger looked up then, saw us, waved us on. And then he sank down on top of his struggling victim.

Neither would rise again.

FIVE

It was nearly nightfall when we finally reached it. The White House. The Great White Wall itself. It rose in the distance like a dream, but its splendor was not diminished when we came right up against it, right there in the moonlight. Quickquick and I had caught up with the Captain in the tulip bed. Captain Mayhap was dismayed upon hearing about Folger, but not destroyed. "He was a fine soldier," he said, in lieu of a eulogy. Still, the White Wall beckoned.

We were more than tired by the time we reached the crawl-space. Quickquick and I thought it prudent to spend the evening in the Great Wall's shadow, and wait until daybreak to enter. But Mayhap was spouting a nervous energy that belied his age and the events of the day. "Bow yer heads, lads," the Captain intoned. "We are about to enter the belly of the beast. Gub rest our souls."

And he went in.

I looked at Quickquick, already curling into sleep. "I have to go," I said. "Folger told me to guard him."

"Then I stay with you," Quickquick said, rousing himself. But he looked so tired. So hungry and tired. He seized on a tiny black box he found hidden by the entrance. "Lucky!" he said. "Food." He offered me some, but I declined. I'd grown past my hungers that day. I'd grown into someone else. And I liked the someone I'd become.

"You eat," I told him. "Stay here. Rest. I'll come back for you soon, and then we can go the whole way together."

And the look he gave me then is one I'll never forget. So tender, so trusting, so kind. Was there ever a more excellent term?

I forged on, calling "Mayhap! Captain!" But he was nowhere to be found. It was as if the Wall itself had consumed him, instead of vice versa. I wandered and wandered, through air ducts and insulation, around honeycombed support beams (clearly we were not the first terms to have had this idea) and over high archways. But no Captain Mayhap.

And everywhere white. White, white, relentlessly white. It made me dizzy after a while. It made me blind. It was all too peaceful. For now that my hungers for life had been piqued, I could never again be sated by merely the absence of hunger. I needed, wanted more. Color. Friendship. Adventures. Love. "Captain Mayhap!" I called again. Again, nothing.

Love or duty? Was that my choice now?

Quickquick or Mayhap? Was it really that simple?

And then I saw him. White as the ghost I thought at first he must be. Splayed out beside a wall sconce, writhing with pleasure. "I have ye now," he ranted. "Ye tried to escape me but ye couldn't. I found ye! Ye're mine! All mine!"

I called out to him once. "Beware, my Captain! Take heed!" His abdomen was distending at an alarming rate, and I feared he might explode. I called again. "For Gub's sake, Mayhap! That Wall will be the end of you!"

He heard me not. He was past hearing. "I have ye!" he kept shouting, engorged but still gnawing at the object of his obsession. He had abandoned all reason, clearly, and I got to him as quickly as I could, but the enormity of his conquest strained at the seams of his lightning-shaped scar. "My Captain!" I shouted, as the seam gave way. White splinters burst through his ganglion. His still-sturdy wings flapped eerily, as in an unseen breeze. But his body, emaciated in life, transformed itself before my very eyes to mere dust on the wall. No question of peeling him off intact. Better to leave him there, his quest fulfilled. He died as he had lived, on his own terms. As his own term.

And I, the realization struck then, was my own term too. I had not failed in my duties. Twice I had saved the Captain. Now it was time to save myself. Quickquick. Love. I bade farewell to the Captain's dusty corpse, then turned my thoughts to Quickquick. I'd already wasted too much time without him. I couldn't get to him swiftly enough. It was my sense of urgency, along with my sense of smell that led me—through one beam to another to another—to Quickquick. To Love. To Life.

I found him curled up beside the tiny black box, same way I left him. How beautiful he looked. "Quickquick?" No answer. Poor thing was so tired. I loved the way he could just let go of the world that way, and sleep. So trusting. So good. So kind. So . . . "Quick-quick?" I smelled it then. Why hadn't I before? What imp of the perverse had gifted me with this finely tuned sense of smell and then ripped it away when I needed it most? "Quickquick!" That little black box had been bait, I saw then. Toxic. Deadly. And I'd told him to eat it. And he'd trusted me. As he trusted everyone. Forgive me, Quickquick. Can you ever forgive me? Forgive me? Would that he had that power again! Could I ever forgive myself?

EPILOGUE

The drama's done. Why then here does any one step forth?—Because one did survive the wreck. Because, like Job, I only am escaped alone to tell thee. Bereft of my friend . . . I am out of words. At last. I feel a lightness that I've never known. A sad but satisfied something has settled in my hindgut and made a home in me. But why Relief feels so much like Emptiness, I know not. What now, Ickishmel? Where now to find my next adventure? Where next to find the words to relate it? I know not this either, though already something is growing within me. New hungers. New wonders. New questions. Like, how tasty is Eve's tree in the Garden of Eden, and is it ever possible to sail back to a land of innocence? Or, how salty is Mrs. Dalloway's basket and are the holes made of memory? Or, how about, how musky is the boat in the Heart of Darkness and does regret rot the floorboards? Or, oh, I know. How bitter is the stake in a vampire's heart? And does Death taint or sweeten its flavor?

I may have to find out. Adventure is calling. Ravishing, ravaging, adventure. And, as the good, brave, loving Quickquick taught me, when adventure calls, there can be no answer but "Yes." Though where my next voyage will lead me, only Fate, bold, daring, and redolent with the tantalizing aroma of—what? Lacewood? Loblolly? Life itself?—can tell.

Notes from the Underground
or The Dream of a Ridiculous Worm

Greatness had eluded me. There had been a time when I bent to it, bent over backwards for it, wriggled away from my warm home, hopeful and expectant, to reach it. And then there had been a time when I wrestled with the jealous fear that someone else might find it and hoard it before me, with the paralyzing thought that I might die before I ever knew it fully. And then finally there had come the time when I writhed in pain, in disappointment, in humiliation, to think that any being as lowly as myself—a worm of the earth, a mere worm, without armor to protect, without color to adorn, without voice or beauty or brilliance—could have ever been so foolish as to hope. But sometimes, amid the wriggling, the wrestling, the writhing, a vision of greatness floated down to me with the rain nonetheless. It was a vague vision, without specifics or particulars. But it felt, sometimes, like music, and now and then it smelled like the pale green roots of the marigolds, or tasted liked the sky-bright blues of my imagination. It sometimes danced inside me, burrowed, as I danced and burrowed inside my warm brown home. But I never could catch it. And always something came between my greatness and my self.

Mud mostly. But also work, friends, progeny, responsibilities. All good things, yes. But small, I thought, compared to greatness.

Daily. Common. Earthbound. When would I take off? When would I find the time? The space? When mud, mud, everywhere mud, filled my days and nights and even my dreams.

But it was something, this mud. It was rich—deep and dark. It was real. And in many ways, I did love its silky hold on me, the way it resisted and supported my every undulation. And I did love the way it shaped my days, as I shaped and reshaped its viscosity. I ate mud, shat mud, slipped and slid and arched into its mud-lusciousness, reproduced in the squishy safety of its mud-womb. I lived in mud and it lived in me, and if greatness existed only far away, up there, in that cold and lonely terror above the top-soil, then I would wriggle and flap my way back down into the mud whenever pitch forks overturned my attentions or sunlight stung my surprised and tender back.

But it was a pitchfork, ironically, that one day prodded me into courage. I found myself suddenly topside, vulnerable and exposed. I understood that I didn't have much time and this understanding distilled the moments I had into something potent and important. Be brave, I told myself. Be brave enough to consider, deeply, the mud-essence of the mud, and the worm-essence of yourself. We did not exist alone, I saw. No one and no world existed by itself. And when I let go of my fear, I saw how the sun warmed the mud. How the rain quenched it and how the marigolds held it and how I, I myself, breathed life into the mud and fed it with my own castings. How the common dance I did, daily, was part of a subterranean greatness, and how the mud I loved was part of other mud, of other earth, that went farther and deeper than I had ever before imagined. It filled up the world and bordered the oceans. And how the earth and the oceans touched the skies and the heavens. And how, when one something touches one something else—how then that first something becomes part of that second. Forever. And how music dances in every shadow, and how fragrance re-imagines every sound—and how you can feel this in the vibrations of the earth, that are touching the oceans, that are touching the skies. And how poetry grows from pale green roots, and how marigolds are still and always marigolds, even when they are not in bloom.

So then I stopped waiting for greatness. I stopped trying to create something immortal because I saw that immortal is part of mortal, not the other way around. And because I could leave my castings as my legacy. And because I am perpetually brushing up against greatness and because everything I touch or smell or see, I am. And because in my world there is no here or there, no then or later, no males or females, no humans or insects, no deaths, no endings. Because there is only this one infinite, uncontainable, interdependent circle of greatness filled with mud and heaven. And earthworms and angels. And me.

Biographical Note

Melody Mansfield's first novel, *The Life Stone of Singing Bird*, was published by Faber and Faber, Inc. to favorable reviews from *The New York Times Book Review*, *Booklist*, and others. Her short fiction, essays, and poetry have appeared in a variety of literary, academic, and commercial publications including *Thought Magazine*, *Inside English*, and *Parents Magazine*. She is currently at work on a number of longer projects, including a semi-autobiographical account of her years as a ballet dancer in New York City. She lives in Los Angeles with her writer/professor husband, Jerry Mansfield, and is the Director of Creative Writing at Milken Community High School.

CPSIA information can be obtained
at www.ICGtesting.com
Printed in the USA
JSHW030228301220
10650JS00001B/24